PRAISE FOR LUCIANA CAVALLARO

The Guardian's Legacy
    Gold Book Award | Literary Titan
    B.R.A.G. Medallion Honouree
    2022 Silver Medal | Global Book Awards
    2022 Finalist | New Film Book Awards
    2021 Finalist | Page Turner Awards
    2021 Quarterfinalist | ScreenCraft Cinematic Book Competition

As with all of Cavallaro's novels, this story includes lots of ancient Greek history and enough action to keep everyone entertained.

— JACQUI MURRAY | FELLOW AUTHOR

Author Luciana Cavallaro has written a gripping action-adventure that promises time travel and teleporting in the series.

— LINNEA TANNER | FELLOW AUTHOR

It's perfect for fans of historical fantasy, teachers who secretly dream of adventure, or anyone who still believes there's magic in the mundane.

— LITERARY TITAN

A modern thriller rooted in the deep soil of ancient myth.

— BOOKVIRAL REVIEW

Can I just say Wow! *The Guardian's Legacy* was so much fun to read and get lost into its world.

— AMAZON REVIEWER

This book was so good! I love a good action adventure story and this is no exception.

— BOOKBUB REVIEWER

This is a story that I had a hard time putting down. I highly recommend this book.

— GOODREADS REVIEWER

THE RACE FOR THE
LOST COIN

THE RACE FOR THE LOST COIN

COIN OF TIME
BOOK TWO

LUCIANA CAVALLARO

Mythos | Publications

Mythos Publications

www.lucianacavallaro.me

Publisher's Note: This is a work of fiction. Names, characters, places, and incidents are a product of the author's imagination. Locales and public names are sometimes used for atmospheric purposes. Any re-semblance to actual people, living or dead, or to businesses, companies, events, institutions, or locales is completely coincidental.

Cover artwork: GetCovers.com

The Race for the Lost Coin / Luciana Cavallaro. — 1st ed.

ISBN 978-0-6452726-6-6

ALSO BY LUCIANA CAVALLARO

Accursed Women: A Collection of Short Stories

Servant of the Gods Series

Search for the Golden Serpent

The Labyrinthine Journey

Minotaur's Lair

Coin of Time Series

The Guardian's Legacy

ACKNOWLEDGEMENTS

To my fearless Advance Reading Team—Rosary, Linnea, Jacqui, Margaret, Lana, Katie, and Charlie—thank you for adventuring with me through time and story.

PRELUDE

'Herakles! Herakles! Are you leaving? What are you hunting? Can we come with you?' Two lithe youths sprinted to catch up with Herakles outside the lion gates of Mycenae.

Herakles didn't slow his pace, the quiver filled with poisoned arrows bouncing against his back. 'I'm off to capture the Erymanthian boar for King Eurystheus. And no, Philotas, you and Alcon cannot come with me.'

'Aw please, Herakles. How are we to become the best hunters if we don't learn from the greatest warrior in all of Hellas?' pleaded Philotas. 'Alcon and I promise to do everything you tell us and we won't get in the way.'

Philotas and Alcon jogged to keep up with the big man, their faces shining with eagerness and adoration.

Herakles glanced at them and shook his head. 'These tasks are mine to complete. Besides, your fathers need you to till the lands to prepare the fields for next season's crops.'

Philotas grimaced, a sheen of perspiration coating his forehead. 'I don't want to be a farmer. I want to be a warrior like you!'

Herakles halted and frowned at the adolescents. 'No, you don't want to be like me. Do you think I enjoy traversing to all points of the earth killing monsters by the order of the king? It's not glorious.' He stepped closer and put a hand on each boy's shoulder. 'When I return, I promise to teach you how to use the bow and arrow.'

'And how to wrestle?' asked Philotas, his eyes wide with hope.

Herakles nodded and gave them a slight smile. 'And how to wrestle.' He indicated back towards the citadel. 'Now off with you both, or it will be dark before I reach Mount Pholoe.' He turned on his heel and resumed walking down the road. From behind him he heard Philotas and Alcon yell and whoop in joy as they ran home.

Hours later, Herakles crossed over the border into Arcadia, home of the centaurs. He stopped by the Erymanthos river, filled his water bag and cupped handfuls of cold liquid and drank his fill. He sat under a tree and leaned against its rough bark. Herakles dug into his knapsack and stilled as his fingers touched a smooth object. He pulled out a stone as big as a duck's egg and lifted it to face level, holding it between his pointer finger and thumb.

'The trouble you have wrought,' he said. 'I wish I hadn't found you on Mount Helicon. I have a mind to secrete you in the deepest cave, away from inquiring minds and treacherous beings like Eurystheus.' He sighed. 'What am I to do with you?'

Herakles was young and brazen during the years he was growing up in the court of his father, Amphitryon, in Thebes. Believing he could bed the mystical muses—after all, he had slept with fifty of King Thespius's daughters at the king's request—he travelled to Mount Helicon searching for the nine muses. He was part way up the mountain when an old crone stopped him and asked if he would help her look for a lost lamb. Not thinking to ask how she had managed to scale the sheer and difficult mountain path, Herakles agreed to help her search for the animal.

He was drawn to a mournful bleating and spied the lamb perched on a rocky outcrop above. Herakles clambered his way up to the animal. His left foot slipped, and he clung to the ledge. He reached out with a hand to gain a firmer hold and pulled himself up onto the ridge.

'Right, come here ...' he said, then he stopped and blinked. The lamb had disappeared.

'Hey there!' he shouted to the old woman and looked down over the ledge to where he had left her. 'What in the name of the gods? Where is the silly woman?' Herakles scanned the way he had come. The woman was nowhere to be seen.

Cursing under his breath, he was about to climb down when he saw an unusual stone. The shape and colour were not something he had seen before. The surface appeared to have been polished by hand, too smooth to be natural. Herakles picked it up. The weight was perfect to be used in a sling, a lethal projectile.

He tossed it into the air. As it rose, a strong wind whipped about his body and his hair stood on end. A flash of lightning streaked across the clear blue sky and the earth trembled.

Herakles caught the stone. He squeezed his eyes shut against the blinding luminescent light. A crack of thunder split the air. Herakles winced and covered his ears. He felt his body hover in the air for a few seconds. He opened his eyes and gaped. Leaves, twigs and loose pebbles scattered as a whirlwind sped towards him and sucked him into its centre. Herakles felt as if his arms and legs were being wrenched from his body. He gritted his teeth, the veins in his arms and legs sticking out like corded rope. He spun through the air, his hair whipping across his face.

Then the wind stopped. Herakles hovered in the air for a moment. He landed on his back with a thud and gasped when his head banged on the hard ground. His mouth watered, bile rising. He drew in a steadying breath and looked around.

'How in the name of Zeus did I get here?' Before him stood the defensive walls of his father's city of Thebes.

Herakles stumbled to his feet and clutched his head. A sharp pain seared its way from the base of his skull to his forehead. It felt as though an axe had cleaved through his head. He heaved, his mouth billowing like the sails on a ship as he purged the contents of his stomach. When his head stopped spinning and the nausea abated, he opened his hand and stared. The stone pulsated and burned, not unlike the embers in a firepit, though it did not leave a mark on his palm. After a few minutes, the stone grew cold.

Had he imagined it all? There was only one way to find out.

Herakles tossed the stone into the air. Lightning flashed and the earth shook. Ear-splitting thunder rocked the air. He sucked in a breath as he was plunged headlong into a fathomless hole.

CHAPTER I

Nik cursed out loud as his head grazed against a dumpster in the dark alleyway outside the hotel, the ancient coin clutched in his hand. His teleportation to escape from his Paris hotel room unseen had left him woozy. He staggered, his sight affected by lingering flashes of light.

He rubbed his forehead. A dull ache, but not the severe pain he had experienced the first time he used the coin to time jump from one place to another. He recalled with a wince landing flat on his back and his head banging on the floor, and then throwing up. The second time jump hadn't been any better, falling forward and smashing his face on the ground. Landing on his feet was a big improvement and he knew that with more practice, he would get better. It was the side effects of teleportation that he wasn't sure about. Some of the earlier guardians mentioned physical impairment, but they weren't clear on what these were and whether the impact was gradual or an accelerated progression into deterioration. Without knowing exactly what his forebearers had experienced, Nik had started making a note of the outcome of each time jump.

His eyesight clearing, Nik opened the palm of his hand and looked down at the coin. There was an imprint of a turtle on one side and, on the obverse, a square split into tiny quadrants, where one contained an image. He believed the pattern had a more significant meaning than his grandfather and former guardians hypothesised. But he wasn't sure whether he fully understood what the icon meant either. In the lower left was the Trinacria, a tiny face from which three legs emerged, bent at the knees, forming a circle. According to his grandfather, the symbol represented the Eastern god Baal, and the three legs signified movement and change.

When the original owner of the stone minted it into two magical coins in the seventh century BCE, they had included the symbol for a reason. The question was, why? Was the image a warning of the potential dangers in using the coin? A reminder of its untold power? But this was not the time to ruminate over the purpose of the image, he needed to get as far away as possible from the hotel.

Nik shoved the coin into his left pocket of his jeans, rebalanced the backpack over his shoulder and peered through the gloom of the alley. He hustled towards the street, pulling his suitcase behind him, the wheels clacking against the uneven surface. Perspiration prickled his forehead, adrenaline coursed through his veins. He headed for Gare Saint-Lazare, the train station he had arranged to have the taxi driver, Sébastien, meet him at 7 pm. He had twenty minutes to spare. Sébastien had picked Nik up as a fare from the airport when he arrived in Paris five days ago and given him his business card.

A mere five days in which his life and his family's world was turned upside down.

Five days of uncertainty, not knowing if his grandfather was alive.

Five days as guardian of the goddess's coin.

Five days to transform and take charge as the guardian.

He rubbed the back of his neck as he maintained a steady pace, not wanting to draw attention to himself. His mind returned to his escape from Konrad Resnik, the rich and powerful Slovakian industrialist. As for Detective Sauveterre, her arrival at the gardens of Musée Rodin had ruined his opportunity to get his grandfather back from the kidnappers. His focus now was to disappear and avoid being found by either of them.

Nik scouted his surroundings taking note of any surveillance cameras. He averted his face as he approached the entry to the underground train station, tucking himself into a discreet corner away from the cameras and out of the main pedestrian thoroughfare. The training with weapons, hand-to-hand combat and the history of the guardianship his grandfather drilled into him was in preparation for situations such as this, except he had not expected a trip to Paris would end in the abduction of his grandfather and a connection to the coin.

Nik thought about his grandfather and the photo Resnik sent him. He searched the pockets in his jacket and his jeans, checked his wallet and riffled through his backpack. His chest tightened and he cursed. The photo must have slipped onto the floor of his hotel room in his haste to leave before the police arrived. He recalled the angry expression on his grandfather's face, and his dishevelled appearance suggested he had put up a bit of a fight. Whatever overtures or demands Resnik made, there was no way his grandfather would tell his captor anything. Nik was concerned Papou may end up either hurt or killed if Resnik decided he was no longer essential. The sooner he had more information about Resnik, the quicker he would find his grandfather.

He heard a car horn, poked his head around the corner and saw Sébastien looking for him. Nik emerged from his location and marched straight for the taxi. The Frenchman leapt out of the car as soon as he saw him.

'*Bonjour! Comment allez-vous aujourd'hui?* How are you today, monsieur?' Sébastien took the suitcase from him and put it into the boot of the car.

'*Bonjour*, Sébastien. I'm fine. Thank you for picking me up.'

'A pleasure, monsieur.'

Nik hopped into the taxi as Sébastien returned to the driver's seat.

'There must be some trouble at the Hilton Paris Opera,' Sébastien commented as he checked his rear-vision mirror and looked over his shoulder before pulling out into the traffic.

'Oh, really?' Nik swallowed. 'Why? What has happened?'

'The police are everywhere. They have blocked the street and rerouted the traffic,' he replied. 'They must be looking for someone.'

Nik rubbed his hands on his thighs. 'What makes you think the police are searching for a person?'

Sébastien shrugged. 'That's what the police do, *non*?' The taxi driver raised a brow at him via the rear-vision mirror.

Nik gave a grim smile. 'Yes, that is what they do.'

'Where do you wish to go?'

CHAPTER 2
MUSÉE RODIN - AFTERMATH OF THE SHOOTING

Blue flashing lights bathed Rue de Varenne, the busy and popular street outside the Musée Rodin, which was blocked off at both ends by police vehicles, the coroner's van, the forensic team and uniformed officers. Detective Alexandrie Sauveterre had briefed the lead detective assigned to the incident and now waited to be dismissed. She leaned against the white police car, scrolled her contacts list on her mobile phone and tapped the call function, ringing her second-in-command.

'Cloutier, any news on our suspect?' Alexandrie narrowed her eyes, foot tapping as she waited for him to update her.

'*Non*, Detective. None of our officers have witnessed him enter or leave the hotel,' replied Cloutier. 'Neither has the hotel staff seen him return.'

'Check with the concierge when Monsieur Zosimos was last sighted,' Sauveterre said rubbing her brow.

'*Droite*. I will call you back.'

Sauveterre hit end call and stared at the blue striations pulsating along the building, the whirling patterns mirroring her frustration and need to track the Australian before the trail was lost. There was movement near the entrance of the musée. Distracted by the activity, she watched the paramedics load the body of Imrich, Konrad Resnik's bodyguard, into the back of the coroner's van. An hour earlier, the forensic team had taken photos and samples from the crime scene. The team now scoured the area where she had overheard Nikolaos and Resnik mention the older Zosimos and a coin. She had followed the Australian to the musée, suspecting he knew more than he had revealed when she questioned him at the hotel. It was fortunate she had, but she wasn't happy about the regrettable outcome. She had shot Imrich when both men resisted being taken into custody for questioning. In the confusion of the shootout, she lost sight of Nikolaos.

She tapped the phone against her thigh, thinking. *Could the abduction of the grandfather and the coin be connected? Is the coin a rare artefact? Have the Zosimoses stumbled onto a black-market syndicate?*

The possibility was credible, the procurement and illegal sale of rare and antique objects that were the must-haves of affluent patrons, and a means to raise money for arms by terrorists' groups and criminal factions. But how did a high school teacher and his grandfather, a retired history professor, fit into the world of the rich Slovakian industrialist Resnik? Were they involved in the black-market trade? Perhaps they were hapless victims due to an unfortunate coincidence or mistaken identity?

Before meeting Nikolaos, Sauveterre ran a background check on both him and his grandfather. Except for a few speeding tickets in his home country, Nikolaos led a nondescript life. His heritage was Greek, his parents were both alive and had been married for thirty years. He had a sister and a large extended family. There were no ties to felonious activities and no connection to international illicit organisations. Both men were lawful citizens, and the elder Zosimos was an esteemed academic. This set-up made little sense. They did not make sense.

The phone vibrated in her hand.

'*Oui*, Cloutier?'

'The receptionist said Monsieur Zosimos paid his account in full earlier this afternoon and he hasn't been back down since.'

'Go to his room, he may still be in there,' Sauveterre said in a clipped tone.

'On my way.'

She heard him tell the receptionist to contact the manager before he ended the phone call. When she had questioned Nikolaos regarding the shops his grandfather visited, he mentioned his grandfather enjoyed searching for antiquities. What if the old man had stumbled across a valuable coin, purchased it and now Resnik desired it? But if Iasos Zosimos had it, why did Resnik want to talk to Nikolaos? If Iasos did not have it and neither did Nikolaos, why agree to meet with the industrialist?

She paced along the street, striding back and forth in front of the coloured striations, the patterns creating a surreal pantomime on her face. She kept checking the phone, wondering what was taking her colleague so long. Five minutes became six, then seven.

'*Mon dieu!* It cannot take that long to find out if the man is still in the hotel!'

Her phone rang.

'*Oui?*'

'Detective, Zosimos is gone. The wardrobe and drawers are empty and there's nothing on the bedside table or on the desk. The two key cards for the room are the only items he left behind.'

'*Merde!*' Sauveterre slapped the wall. Two police officers standing nearby gave her a wary look.

'The hotel has security cameras. I'm going to check the footage for this floor and the stairwells.' Cloutier paused. 'Is Zosimos dangerous?'

'*Non*, but he is a person of interest. He may be our only link to his grandfather's disappearance.' Sauveterre bit her bottom lip. 'Don't let anyone into the room. I want to look around.'

'I will see to it. How much longer will you be?'

'Perhaps another hour. You know how it is with investigations involving police shootings.'

'*Oui*. I'll seal the room and review the security footage until you arrive.'

'Very good. Let's hope you find something that will indicate where he's gone.' Sauveterre ended the call, slid the phone into her jacket pocket and went back into the gardens. She tracked down the lead detective.

'What is it, Sauveterre?' he asked.

'My witness has disappeared. I must leave and join my team at the hotel where he was staying,' she replied.

'Hmm ... I understand he is a high school teacher and not a criminal mastermind, *oui?* How did he manage to elude your officers?'

Sauveterre bristled. 'That's what I intend to find out. And though he may be a high school teacher, he possesses information regarding the abduction of his grandfather and is essential to my investigation.'

The detective threw his hands up in mock defence. 'Don't get so uptight, Sauveterre. I have no further need for you. Go and get your elusive teacher, another failed attempt to keep a man.'

'You're an arsehole, Bouchard. As if you have an impressive record of retaining partners. No-one wants to work with you, let alone sleep with you,' said Sauveterre, her lip curled. 'Oops.' She covered her mouth, then dropped her hand. 'Did I say that out loud?'

'Fuck you, Sauveterre.' Bouchard's face turned an angry red.

'I'll pass on the offer, I've more promising propositions to choose from,' Sauveterre mocked and spun on her heel.

'That's not what I hear! Besides, you couldn't handle a man like me, Sauveterre!' shouted Bouchard.

Sauveterre clenched her hands and told herself to keep walking. Dealing with the likes of Bouchard, who did his utmost to undermine her authority, steeled her resolve to be the best detective in the French police force. She reminded herself, as one of the youngest detectives she had the highest number of solved cases and arrests in her division. Bouchard, with his machismo and arrogance, did not have the aptitude or innate skills required to solve complex crimes.

The spiteful and chauvinistic insults were not daily occurrences, but they did happen, and she tended to ignore them. Some days, the bullying was difficult not to take personally and from experience she knew speaking out would not help. The one occasion she had reached out to her superior regarding the sexist innuendos and denigrating comments, the taunts escalated. Never again did she report the narcissistic and offensive behaviour.

She withstood the harassments from her days at the police academy where she outshone her classmates. A training officer had pulled her aside and explained the difference between her and her fellow cadets. Her fortitude and attitude to never give up, and the desire to triumph for her parents, were the reasons she worked so hard to achieve justice for victims of crimes. He told her to focus on her duties and stay away from the politics of policing. He later became her mentor and stoutest supporter, encouraging her to exceed where others failed.

Sauveterre beckoned a young police officer as she crossed the road to a police vehicle.

'*Oui*, Detective?'

'Drive me to the Hilton Paris Opera.'

'*Oui*, Detective.'

The police officer ran around the car to the driver's side and hopped in. Sauveterre was buckling the seat belt when her phone rang again. She frowned as she recognised the number.

'*Bonjour*, Commissioner.'

'Detective Sauveterre, come to my office, now.'

'Commissioner, I am on my way to conduct a search—' Sauveterre began.

'Your second-in-command can take the lead. My secretary will inform me as soon as you arrive.' The police commissioner hung up.

'*Merde!*' Sauveterre punched the side panel of the door. The police officer flinched, glancing at her startled.

'Take me to the Prefecture,' she snapped.

The police officer indicated to turn right at the next intersection. Sauveterre rapped her fingers on the armrest. The commissioner ringing her direct was unusual. Must be important if he rang and not his secretary.

Some twenty minutes later, they turned into the driveway of the Prefecture. The officer stopped at the security gate and rolled down the window.

Sauveterre leaned over to peer at the sentry on duty and flashed her badge. '*Bonjour*, Katia.'

The officer's eyes lit up. '*Bonjour*, Detective Sauveterre.' She turned to her fellow guards and waved at them to lift the boom gate. 'Have a good evening, Detective.'

'*Merci. Au revoir.*'

Her driver parked the vehicle in an empty bay, in a row of patrol cars. Sauveterre turned to him and paused before opening her door.

'*Merci.*'

The young officer smiled. 'You are welcome, Detective.'

'What is your name?'

'Étienne Tolbert.'

'Étienne, wait here. I'll need you to drive me to the hotel once I have finished my meeting with the commissioner.'

'*Bien sûr.*'

Sauveterre nodded and got out of the car. She gazed at the nineteenth-century structure, an imposing building with a long history in law enforcement dating back to 1800. Since its conception, the Prefecture de Police had protected the citizens of Paris from petty crimes and disasters to the most violent of offences, including terrorism. When Alexandrie started out as a cadet, she vowed to honour her deceased parents, doing her utmost to preserve their memory and to prevent acts of extremism.

She still remembered the day she and her sister, Claudette, learned of their parents' deaths. For Alexandrie, 11 September 2001 changed her life, and she vowed to do her part to protect innocent people from radicals and violent individuals.

The start of a car engine brought her back to the present. Alexandrie glanced over her shoulder, seeing a vehicle leave. She drew in a deep breath, walked across the car park and entered the building. She headed for the elevator. On the ride up to the police commissioner's floor, she considered various reasons why he would summon her without notice.

She frowned. From previous experiences the commissioner was upfront and allowed his detectives to work independently and with little interference. This sudden directive was out of character.

The old elevator shuddered to a stop, and Alexandrie stepped out. The police commissioner's secretary saw her, picked up the phone, spoke a few brief words, and placed the phone back on the receiver.

'Go right in, the commissioner is expecting you,' said the secretary with a flick of her head.

Alexandrie turned the doorknob and pushed open the heavy oak door. 'Good evening, Commissioner, I under—' she hesitated, seeing two men sitting in front of the commissioner's large rectangular walnut coloured desk.

The commissioner beckoned her. 'Come in, Detective Sauveterre.'

Alexandrie closed the door behind her and sat on an empty chair alongside the two men.

'Detective, this is Commander Dufort and Agent Janssens from Interpol,' introduced the commissioner. 'They have been tracking your Australian and, in particular, his grandfather for the past month. In the interest of both investigations, Commander Dufort and I thought it beneficial for our lead officers to collaborate. You and Agent Janssens will work together. This case is bound to attract international attention and we must be unified in our search for the older Australian.'

'Commissioner, I have a good team of people working on this case and I don't need anyone else. No offence to Agent Janssens, who I'm sure is a capable investigator,' she said sitting upright, hands clenched on her lap.

The police commissioner's mouth drew into a taut line. 'Detective Sauveterre, this is not a request. You will share your Intel with Agent Janssens, he will provide information Interpol has on the two men.'

Alexandrie ground her teeth. She knew there was no chance of manoeuvring out of this predicament but couldn't help herself. 'Just so we are clear: Nikolaos Zosimos reported his grandfather missing to the police and I—' she pointed at herself '—am the lead detective. If we are to work together, I want all the paperwork, *all* of it, and not just fragments as a token gesture of goodwill.'

'Detective ... ' the police commissioner's brown eyes glinted.

Commander Dufort raised his hand. '*Tout va bien, je comprends.* Detective Sauveterre, I do not have a problem revealing what Intel we have on the older Zosimos, but there are details from our investigation we cannot disclose.'

Alexandrie sat back and folded her arms across her chest. 'Then we are at an impasse. For one, I know Konrad Resnik is involved, as are the neo-Nazis.'

The two Interpol agents exchanged glances.

'How do you know about Resnik and the neo-Nazis?' Dufort asked.

Alexandrie shook her head. '*Non.* Your turn to part with some valuable intelligence.'

'Iasos Zosimos visited several neo-Nazi shop-fronts—'

'Bah, I already know this,' Alexandrie said with a sniff and flicked her hand, as if shooing a fly.

Dufort turned to Janssens. 'Show the detective the photo.'

Janssens reached for a well-worn brown leather briefcase next to him on the floor and pulled out a photo. He held it out to Alexandrie. She gazed at the scene and plucked the snapshot from his fingers to study it.

'The man on the right is Iasos Zosimos, and the other man is —' Dufort started to say.

'I know who the other man is: Imrich, Resnik's bodyguard. I shot him tonight,' said Alexandrie, her voice flat. She handed the photograph back to Janssens.

Silence filled the room.

'What you do not know is that Monsieur Zosimos met him in Marseilles,' Dufort said.

Alexandrie shrugged. 'All you have is a photo of two men outside a shop. Did they exchange money? Or anything else? How long did they speak? Did you hear what they spoke about? That is, if they talked at all.'

Dufort leaned back in his chair, a finger tapping on the

armrest. 'You are, of course, correct. They did not speak, nor did they exchange money or papers. But the fact remains that both men were at the same shop within minutes of each other.'

'Perhaps,' Alexandrie nodded. 'However, I don't believe it was a coincidence that Herr Imrich showed up at the same time as Monsieur Zosimos. What I have deduced is that Iasos Zosimos did not know the man, that much is clear from his expression in the photo. Having visited the shop and questioned the store owner, the elder Australian was leaving when Herr Imrich arrived.' She glanced at the commissioner, noticing his jaw was working back and forth, as if masticating a chewy piece of meat. She turned back to the Interpol agents.

'You came here, I didn't seek you out. It's obvious you want something from me, something specific. If that is so, then the only way for this partnership to work—' she waved her hand in a circle encompassing all four of them '—is to cooperate and communicate what you know and any evidence you've found.'

She waited, and when there was no response, she stood.

'Thank you, gentlemen.'

Alexandrie left the commissioner's office. She expected she would have to explain her behaviour to her superior later, but she also knew he would defend her stance regarding the investigation. Her track record of solving cases was a testament to her ability to search, find clues, and corroborate information in the most unlikely avenues.

CHAPTER 3

Alexandrie stomped across the car park to where her driver and other new graduate constables were milling about, smoking and laughing.

'Étienne!'

The young patrolman jumped, the cigarette tumbling from his lips. He shooed his companions away and spun around, straightening his sky-blue shirt and adjusting his bullet-proof vest.

'Drive me to the Hilton Paris Opera.' She yanked the door open, got into the car and tapped away on her phone. 'Cloutier ... I am on my way. Have you discovered anything new?'

'*Oui* ... a photo of an older man bound to a chair.'

Alexandrie paused to process it all. 'How did that piece of evidence get missed by forensics when they processed the room?'

'I don't know,' Cloutier replied angry. 'Such incompetence is unacceptable.' She heard him give terse instructions to other officers on their team. 'One of our people found the picture under the bed. We are lucky the cleaners didn't vacuum too well under there.'

'Étienne, get that siren going,' she ordered, and then said to her second-in-command, 'Cloutier, take possession of the security footage for that floor.'

'We've examined the video, and there are no further images of the Australian after he left to meet Konrad Resnik.'

'He had to return after the incident at Rodin's Musée. There must be some footage of him.'

'I'll re-examine the recordings again. I had our team check every floor, room and stairway, and he isn't here.'

Alexandrie pursed her lips. How did Nikolaos Zosimos elude her and her team? One minute he was in her sights and then he disappeared, nowhere to be found. Before sending Cloutier and their team to the hotel, they had combed the grounds searching for him. Word of his getaway had spread quicker than wildfire and Bouchard's dig at not keeping a man rankled more than she wished.

'Get every tape and footage for the day, Cloutier. If the hotel security doesn't provide the material, charge them with obstruction.' She sensed Étienne's glance when she hung up. 'What?'

'It's not your fault the suspect got away.'

'I am the lead detective, and all responsibility falls to me. Nikolaos Zosimos is not a felon, he has done nothing wrong, however he knows a great deal about the abduction of his grandfather, and that is why we must find him,' she said, staring out of the windscreen.

Thirty minutes later, they pulled up outside the Hilton hotel. Alexandrie was halfway out the door when she swung back to the constable.

'Best you come along if you want experience in field work.' She got out of the car, but not before she saw the broad grin on Étienne's face.

They entered the hotel, Alexandrie striding straight for the reception desk and flashing her badge.

'Where is Detective Cloutier?'

'He's with our hotel security manager. I will take you to them.'

The woman spoke a few words to her co-worker and led Alexandrie and Étienne to the elevator. When they reached the basement floor, the concierge showed them to the surveillance room where Cloutier and the head of security were watching video recordings.

Sauveterre beckoned her partner. Cloutier acknowledged her with a nod, had a quick word to the security officer and came out to join her and Étienne in the corridor.

'I've just come from the commissioner's office.' The detective's eyes flashed. 'He has instructed me to share information from our investigation with Agent Janssens from Interpol.'

Cloutier swore. 'And take the glory when we've done all the work? Arseholes. They should leave proper police work to us and go—'

'Forget it for now and talk me through what you've found. We'll deal with Janssens later.' She nodded at the image on the screen where the security guard sat waiting. They walked into the room. 'What do you have to show me?'

'It could be him,' Cloutier said, pointing, 'although we aren't sure. The image is too blurry to make out his features. But first, I want you to see this footage from the previous day. He exits a room that wasn't his. What he does next is most peculiar. He disappears for a few seconds and then goes into the lift.' He tapped the head of security on the shoulder. 'Pull up that shot we were examining earlier.'

Alexandrie leaned in, peering at the screen. 'What *is* he doing?' She watched Nikolaos Zosimos stand outside the door of his room and look around. He appeared to change his mind and headed down the corridor, where he was out of the shot for a few minutes, and then as Cloutier confirmed, came back into view and got into the elevator. 'He doesn't look well.' She tapped the screen, noticing the sheen on his forehead. 'What is at the end of the passage?'

The security chief shrugged. 'More suites.'

'Show Detective Sauveterre the other film,' instructed Cloutier. 'This shot is where we can't determine if this is Zosimos.'

Alexandrie studied the clip. The time stamp and date fit the parameters of the approximate period Nikolaos allegedly returned to the hotel, though, as her partner mentioned, the video capture of the person was indistinct. Something caught her attention and she moved closer, squinting at the screen.

'Can you go back a few seconds?' she asked the security guard.

'*Oui*, Detective.'

A moment passed while she scanned the screen. 'Stop there. Is that his room with the bright light flickering?' She tilted her head to one side.

Cloutier checked the room number. '*Oui*, that was Zosimos's suite.'

'It looks like flashing light bulbs from an old camera,' commented Étienne, hands on his hips.

'Play it back,' Alexandrie ordered. 'Are you able to slow that section of the clip?'

'Of course.' The security officer rewound the footage, set the speed to the slowest function and pressed play.

'Stop.' Alexandrie stooped to study the frame.

'Is that a shadow of a person in the room?' asked Cloutier, stunned.

'It could be. Looks like a human figure but I want to know where that flash came from,' she said. 'Were there any traces of broken glass, filament or anything unusual in the room?'

Cloutier shook his head. 'Nothing. It was clean, except for the photo.'

'Let me see it.'

Cloutier handed her the snapshot sealed in a plastic evidence bag. Alexandrie studied the man bound to a chair, and despite his bedraggled appearance, his body language and facial expression showed anger, not fear. She could also see the familial resemblance between Nikolaos and his grandfather.

She turned to the guard. 'Give a copy of the footage of what we've seen to the constable. I want to see the floor and room now. I also want to know who occupied the room next door to Zosimos and if he knew them.'

'Of course ...' Cloutier started to say.

Alexandrie was out the door before Cloutier completed his sentence, the others slow to react. Her second-in-command hurried to catch up as she approached the elevator.

'I'm not sure what else there is to find. The room was cleaned,' said Cloutier.

'Lucky for us they didn't do a great job,' she said. 'We cannot afford any more mistakes, not now that we have evidence of an international guest in our country being held hostage.'

'I've had words with the leader of the forensics.' Cloutier shoved a hand in his jacket pocket. 'It's odd how the grandson has vanished. He's here alone, doesn't know anyone or have contacts that we're aware of in Paris, and his family in Greece has not heard from him. Where the hell is he? He's a freakin' schoolteacher, how does he just disappear?'

'Nikolaos Zosimos and his grandfather came here for a purpose, not for a holiday. We solve that puzzle, we find the two men. I can guarantee the younger Zosimos is searching for his grandfather and won't leave until he has found him,' she said.

The elevator doors opened and she stepped out into the passageway, noting the camera's position, the stairwell, and the proximity to the suite the Australian occupied. Cloutier walked ahead of her and unlocked the door. Alexandrie pulled on black nitrile gloves and examined the door and the door-jambs. She dabbed a finger against the frame and rubbed her thumb and finger, her fingertips oily.

'Call the forensic team back. I want the door and door frame checked for particulates. Have them dust for prints on the pot and stand at the end of the hallway.'

She entered the room, her gaze sweeping across the furniture, and crossed over to the wardrobe where the room safe was situated. The door to the safe was ajar. She opened it further and felt around inside, pulling up the corners of the felt mat. She went into the bathroom. Fresh new bottles and wrapped bars of soap replaced all the used toiletries. The fragrance of the soap reminded her of her first meeting with Nikolaos, and how she was caught off guard by his good looks, the timbre of his voice and the electric charge from their handshake. Her heart did a flip as an unbidden vision of Nikolaos surfaced with wet hair and a towel wrapped around his waist.

'Sauveterre, the forensics are returning. Should be here in about fifteen ... twenty minutes,' Cloutier called out.

'Good.' Alexandrie frowned at her reflection. She clenched her hands and gave herself a mental shake before joining Cloutier.

CHAPTER 4

Nik instructed Sébastien to drop him off along Quai de Grenelle in the Left Bank province. The Frenchman turned to Nik as he was about to pay the fare. Gone was the smiling and affable driver, his expression replaced by a concerned countenance.

'Be careful, *monsieur*. Our Police Nationale and Gendarmerie Nationale are powerful, protective of their citizens and fearless, and have extensive resources. They will not give up.' He scribbled on a card and passed it to Nik. 'You call me on this private number, and I will come.'

'Sébastien—' Nik shook his head.

'*Monsieur*, I know good people when I meet them, and you are a respectable person. You ring and I'll come.'

'*Merci beacoup*, and call me Nik.'

Sébastien nodded. They shook hands, and the Frenchman got out of the car.

Nik took a moment to digest the brief conversation before opening his door. Sébastien had set his suitcase on the sidewalk. Nik waited until the taxi had merged into the traffic, engulfed by the fast-flowing vehicles before walking to Les Jardins d'Eiffel, his new hotel.

When he got into his room, he sorted his belongings, and secured his weapons in the safe. He placed his laptop on the desk, pulled out his toiletry bag and put it in the bathroom, and then ordered room service. The last meal he had was lunch the previous day, over thirty hours ago. He flopped onto the bed and stared at the ceiling. What a crazy turn of events. No-one would believe him if he told them about being hunted by the police and threatened by a neo-Nazi. Such incidents did not happen to ordinary people like him.

The following day, around midday, Nik went to the Eiffel Tower. He wanted to hide amid the multitude of tourists and do a little research in one of the cafés. Plus, he needed to get out of the confines of the hotel room. He felt constricted and desired to be surrounded by people, even if they were strangers.

Nik joined the queue to purchase a ticket to the second floor of the tower. As the line progressed, he scanned the crowd, and despite the recent terrorist attacks in the city some months ago, people from around the world still came in the thousands. His pulse raced and his mouth went dry seeing the gendarme on the outer fringes of the tower's structure. Nik lowered his head and angled his body away from the constabulary. A few minutes later, someone tapped him on the shoulder.

Crap. Nik stiffened.

'*Bonjour*, ah ... the line is moving there, fella,' a male voice prompted from behind him.

'Right.' Nik nodded and took a few steps to close the gap, keeping his face averted.

'Oh, you speak English. Are you from England?' the man asked in a jovial tone.

'No, Australia,' Nik replied, then kicked himself for giving away his nationality. A mistake he wouldn't make again.

'Hey sweetheart, this man is an Aussie.' The man jutted out his hand. 'My name is Dan, and this is my wife, Gloria. We are from Ohio.'

Nik shook the man's hand and nodded at his wife, thinking of a way to extricate himself from the over-friendly couple. 'My name is ... John.'

'Amazing piece of architecture, isn't it?' Dan pointed at the iron structure. 'Hard to believe the Parisians were going to pull it down in 1909.'

'It's very impressive,' Nik agreed. 'Hitler wanted to dismantle it but never got the chance. The French resistance fighters cut the cables to the elevator.'

'Glad they didn't,' said Gloria, 'or we wouldn't be here lining up to take a gander at it.'

'Quite.' Nik sneaked a look across the vast grounds of the Eiffel Tower, checking the whereabouts of the police.

'Are you here on your own?' asked Dan.

'Pardon?' Nik blinked, his mind racing.

'Are you holidaying on your own?' Dan repeated, shaking his head in commiseration. 'A shame, being in the city of romance and all alone.'

'And such a good-looking young man,' commented Gloria, with a twinkle in her eyes.

'Oh ... ah ... well.' Nik coughed, his cheeks reddening. 'I'm here on business and taking a day off to see the sights.' The queue moved and Nik followed with the two Americans close behind.

'What sort of business are you in? I used to travel for work, right across the country, didn't I, sweetheart? A financial investigator, checking on companies and examining documents and reports to make sure they were accurate, and all their records verified and legitimate. Sure did a lot of miles.'

Gloria smacked her husband on the arm. 'Leave the poor man alone and stop nattering at him. John is here to take a break from work and doesn't need to listen to you prattle on.'

'That's okay,' said Nik, shuffling along in the slow-moving line.

'There you go, sweetheart, he doesn't mind. How long are you in Paris for?'

'Just a few days.'

'What work did you say you do?'

'I didn't.'

Nik reached the ticket counter and handed over twenty euro that granted him access to the second level. He took the ticket and walked through the gate. He nodded at the American couple and sped towards the lifts. Once in the elevator, Nik slipped the ticket into his jeans pocket. The second level had numerous restaurants and gift shops, each unique and stylistic in design. The ticket allowed him access to the top of the tower, though he had to climb the stairs from level one to the second level and take the lift the rest of the way.

On the ride up to the first floor, Nik's thoughts went to the incident at Rodin's Musée. He presumed Resnik managed to get himself out of trouble following the shooting. As to Detective Sauveterre, was she looking for him? He clenched his hands, irritated she had shown up and ruined his opportunity to get his grandfather back. Her appearance wasn't a total surprise, however, given her earlier efforts in tailing him to Marseilles and later confronting him at the hotel.

Nik scaled the iron staircase with the throng, shifting his backpack from one shoulder to the other, the weight of his laptop bumping against his back. The animated chatter in different languages washed over him as he threaded his way through the tourists, ignoring the panoramic and magnificent expanse of Paris. He paused on the landing of the first floor, the volume of excited voices bringing him back to the present. It was then he noticed the glass floor. He glanced down to the grounds below where hundreds of tourists gathered, walking about and taking photos.

On another occasion, Nik would have taken the time to admire the elegant structure and be impressed by the engineering ingenuity used to construct such an object of beauty. But the pleasures of sightseeing would have to wait, finding his grandfather was more pressing, as was researching Resnik's background and his purpose for wanting the coins. Nik rubbed the back of his neck. *Could the Slovakian industrialist already have the sister coin and sought its sibling?*

Before the coins were created, they had existed as a piece of stone and once belonged to Herakles. It was he, who by chance, had discovered the power the stone manifested. Herakles had never disclosed exactly what the power was, and passed the stone on to his son with strict instructions never to use it and for future generations to protect it with their lives. When he died, so did the secret of the stone. From the conversations Nik had with his grandfather and what he had gleaned from the various ancient sources, it seemed that the combined power of the coins was greater than the volcanic eruption that wiped out the entire civilisation on ancient Thera.

Nik knew from experience that one coin could teleport a person from place to place, but prior knowledge of the location and what it looked like was essential for a successful time jump. There was a certain skill to using the coin, one that he was learning to control. What concerned him was what else it could do, and Resnik's desire to possess both coins. *Did he know the power they could wield?*

Troubled by that thought, Nik crossed the glass floor and

scaled the staircase. He must find the second coin before Resnik does.

The second floor of the tower showcased all of Paris in her splendour, but Nik again disregarded the clear views of the capital's monuments and made a beeline for the bistro. Stepping through the door, he reeled at the sound of clinking china, crying children and the raised voices of harried parents. The clamour reminded him of the school grounds where he taught and boisterous teenage boys running around kicking a football, playing basketball or shouting over each other for attention. It was a weird experience, that the general hubbub of a school was reflected in such a majestic city and on an iconic piece of architecture.

Nik found a table in a corner, took out his laptop and noted the free wi-fi access printed on the bottom of the menu. A few seconds passed as it connected and then he opened the *Tor* browser. Another one of his grandfather's strategies in protecting the coin, the *Tor* browser provided security and anonymity while searching the internet, which was used by some criminal factions to hide their communications and dealings. Nik typed 'Resnik' and 'neo-Nazi' into the search bar and waited as the terms ping-ponged from one encrypted server to another, bouncing off multiple satellites. A smiling waitress approached his table, and he used a mix of French and English to order a coffee, a bottle of mineral water and burger with a side of fries.

Nik returned to the findings on the screen, clicked on various links and skimmed the information. There was no direct link between Resnik and the neo-Nazi movement, other than a few references to branches of far-right extremists moving to and working in Canada, Australia and a number of European countries. Law agencies in Europe and North America had banned four neo-Nazi groups, yet they had set up operations in Australia with no issues.

Nik rapped his fingers on the table and pursed his lips. He typed in 'Konrad Resnik' and a list of articles mentioning the wealthy magnate popped up on the screen. Nik navigated to some sites and made notes. As he delved deeper into the research, he came across information about Heinrich Himmler and his fascination with relics. He had overseen an organisation called *The Ahnenerbe*, which was dedicated to a wide range of scholarly and scientific research that attracted the academic elite of Nazi Germany.

A shadow fell over him. He looked up at the waitress who placed his order on the table.

'*Merci beaucoup*,' he said. She smiled and moved away.

Nik leaned back in his chair, staring at the screen and considering the information. He shut the laptop, stowed it away into his backpack and ate his meal, thinking about what to do next.

CHAPTER 5

Nik returned to the hotel. Les Jardins d'Eiffel was modest in comparison to the Hilton Opera Hotel, the rooms were smaller and it was easy to bump into the furniture. He didn't dare use the coin to teleport to and from the room as chances were he'd injure himself on arrival. With time and practice he'd improve, neither of which he had an opportunity to test. He would just have to deal with the consequences of using the coin. He sat on the bed and skimmed through his research notes, going back and forth to the websites he had bookmarked.

Nik stood, and stretched his back and neck. He decided not go out again so soon, not wanting to risk being identified by the police. There was nothing on the newsfeed to suggest the police were looking for him but given Detective Sauveterre had some of her officers tail him to Marseilles, the odds were a possibility. He flopped onto the bed and thought back to what his grandfather told him about the history of the coin and how they were bound to protect it from being discovered.

The greatest surprise for him was how the legacy of the coin had been kept a well-guarded secret and part of his family's history for thousands of years, where only one person ever knew of its existence—*The Guardian*. His grandfather would only tell him the story after he accepted the role of being the coin's next protector. Even now, knowing what he did about the coin and his family's duty to protect it, the truth sounded too surreal, like an action-adventure movie with a hero like Indiana Jones seeking rare and powerful artefacts. He wondered what Steven Spielberg would make of this real-life enigma, a supernatural object that teleported a person from place to place.

Herakles was the first owner and guardian of the stone, and centuries later someone had minted the two coins from it. Prior to the coins' manufacture, the stone fell into the guardianship of Helen of Sparta, where one of Nik's ancestors, a warrior, came back from Troy with King Menelaos and Helen, and had become her bodyguard. From that first association the two families were bound.

After Helen died, the stone was passed on to future descendants until it became too dangerous for it to remain in Sparta, and was given to the bodyguard. He was instructed to return 'when two kings, one of them a lion' was born. The bodyguard fled to Aegina, where he converted the stone into two coins. Centuries later, King Leonidas, the warrior-king—the 'lion' as foretold by the Oracle—and who led the Spartan warriors into battle at Thermopylae against the Persians, was given the coins.

From the information his grandfather had amassed from ancient sources, one of the coins disappeared during the battle. That was when the king entrusted the sister coin to the bodyguard. King Leonidas instructed him to go to Ithaka and give the coin to the descendant of Odysseus. The warrior did as ordered and the king of Ithaka took him on as his own personal bodyguard. A decade later, shortly after seeing unknown petitioners, the king was killed, and the coin disappeared. The bodyguard was at home at the time of the king's death, his wife giving birth. When he heard what happened, he spent days questioning people closest to the king and the countless slaves who worked in the palace. He searched the island and then left his family and Ithaka to track down the coin.

How the bodyguard found the coin was a mystery; there were no written records on how he located and retrieved the coin. Since then, for the past two thousand years, the coin had remained with the Zosimos family as its guardians.

Nik sat up. It was important he wrote down the effects he experienced from teleporting. He wanted to keep a record of any physical and psychological changes using the coin will have in the short term and long term. Knowing how the coin works and the impact it has would be useful. He'd have a better understanding of what to expect and future guardians could be forewarned. Although, maybe Herakles was right about keeping the power of the coins a secret. He shook his head. No. Best the information was shared and the dangers in using the coins understood.

He thought about his first experimental attempt in using the coin, which he had based on Herodotos' application of the coin. When Nik time jumped, he arrived in his own home and not in Papou's bunker. Throughout the teleportation, he felt as if his limbs were being pulled apart, almost like having his arms and legs wrenched all at once. Then there was the arrival, like a baby being born, squished out from a small aperture and thrust unceremoniously into another location. Nik rubbed the back of his head. A slight bump remained from having landed flat on his back and banging his head on the floor of his living room. It was difficult to believe this had happened only a few days earlier, what with everything that had since happened, it felt like he'd been in Paris much longer than five days. Thankfully, he improved with each time jump, learning to focus on particular features of a destination and landing on his feet.

He took the coin out of his pocket and frowned, hoping it would reveal something, anything, that would help him learn its secrets. One thing he did know, his grandfather would be unhappy with him if he found out Nik used the coin. He would deal with his grandfather's outrage later but for now, it was vital he learned more about Konrad Resnik; what drove him, why he wanted the coins, how he intended to use them, and crucially, how he had found out about the precious heirlooms.

Nik required more details than the Internet could provide, and that of the dark web search on *Tor*, to create a comprehensive profile on Europe's richest man. The one computer system with the highest level of security and unidentifiable ISP was back at his grandfather's place in Perth. But to jump back and forth without further knowledge of the risks of the side effects might be more detrimental than remaining in hiding in Paris. Hacking into the Interpol database or national police computer banks was not one of Nik's skills. Searching and researching, yes. Advanced weapons usage and hand-to-hand combat, yes. But he was not a black hat hacker.

Time to plan what to do next and decide who could help him.

CHAPTER 6

Nik emerged from the bathroom with a towel wrapped around his waist, and checked his laptop. Fifty per cent battery life. He sat on the bed, picked up his mobile, opened his favourite's contact list and tapped a phone number into his new Android.

'Hi, Dad.'

'Hi there, Nik. Did you get a new phone number?'

'Ah ... yes, I dropped my mobile and it broke, so I had to get a new one,' lied Nik. 'How are you doing?'

'A little frustrated. I've called the Department of Foreign Affairs to get advice and what they can do to find Papou. They've communicated with the Australian Embassy in Paris, who are going to contact their French counterpart to get answers on what they are doing, and they'll get back to us,' replied his father, his voice tense. 'That silly old bastard! Why he didn't wait until the end of school term so you could both fly out together. He shouldn't have gone alone, not at his age. What was so important that he had to leave before you finished school?'

'He wanted to do some family research,' answered Nik. 'Besides, Papou is fit and quite youthful for his age, Dad.'

'In France?' His father's tone came across as incredulous. 'We don't have family or any familial ties with France. Our ancestry is as Greek as you can get. The doddering old fool has caused nothing but grief and you shouldn't be the one dealing with this trouble.'

'I believe Papou found an ancestor from the Mediaeval period who had travelled to Marseilles. He wanted to learn why our ancestor voyaged to the city and what he did while there. Plus the other reason for the trip was that Marseilles was founded by the Ionian Greeks in six hundred BCE, and Papou couldn't resist going there to take a look at the museum as well,' said Nik. He did not enjoy lying to his father or his mother, and while it was true his grandfather went to Marseilles, he felt it best to tell part of the truth to give the pretext more credence.

'Regardless of the reason why Papou went there, he should have waited until you joined him. Have you learned anything new from the police?' his father asked in a weary voice.

Nik hung his head. 'No, I haven't had an update from the police, other than they are expanding their search.'

'What does that mean? Do they think he's dead?' His father's voice was panicky.

Nik bit his bottom lip. 'I really don't know, Dad. I guess they must consider all factors with missing persons.'

There was silence.

'How are Mum and Chara?'

'Quite upset. They want to fly over.'

'I understand, but there is no point coming to Paris. There's not a great deal to do but sit around and wait for news,' Nik said, thinking fast. 'I've been to Marseilles, the last place he was sightseeing, and I plan to go back there to revisit the antique store he went to before disappearing.'

'You be careful, Niko.'

Nik swallowed back the lump in his throat. His dad called him 'Niko' on rare occasions. 'I'm always careful, Dad.'

His father cleared his throat. 'Okay. Phone when you get more news.'

'Of course. I'll ring as soon as I hear anything.' Nik nodded. 'Bye, Dad.'

'Bye, Nik.'

Nik hung up and dropped his phone on the bed and exhaled with frustration. His mind kept running over details of the information he acquired that afternoon at the Eiffel Tower. He picked up the business card Sébastien gave him and stared at the number. He put the card on the desk and reached for the hotel phone to dial for room service. He then pulled on his jeans and a black t-shirt.

While he waited for his dinner, Nik flipped open his laptop and checked the news stream to see if there were any articles or snippets from the police. He frowned as he scrolled through the headlines, clicking on a link when a news headline caught his attention. There was no news item about the shooting incident at the museum.

Nothing.

He thought reporters would have picked up some bulletin from the police about the shooting and he half expected to see Detective Sauveterre's picture or a statement from her. The confrontation between Imrich, Resnik's lieutenant, and the detective didn't go well in spite of the latter's warning to the terrorist at drawing a weapon on a police officer. Nik bit the inside of his cheek, recalling blood spurting from Imrich's forehead, the detective's precision marksmanship saving him from being shot by the German.

He tapped his mouth with a finger and wondered why the police were withholding the information. As there had been a fatality, he was surprised that not a single news outlet reported what had happened given how quickly information is posted on the internet. Or were they ordered to withhold from releasing the news? If they were, then the police were planning something big. Apprehension clawed at his gut, sharp and acute.

Nik reached into his jeans front pocket and pulled out the coin. For such a small object, it had caused so much havoc. Knowing the power of the coin and what it could do, he shuddered to think what chaos two coins used together could manifest. If only Herakles had disclosed what he experienced with the stone when it was in its original form. Must have been horrifying for the legendary warrior, as he had chosen not to reveal what happened to him when he used it. Nik's thoughts turned to his close encounter with the industrialist and enforcer. The question he kept mulling over was how did Resnik discover the existence of the coins?

Nik turned on the television and flicked through the stations. Again, there was no report on the shooting incident on any of the networks. A chill ran up his spine. The absence of news did not given him any comfort. Startled by a sharp rap on the door, Nik got up and peered through the peephole. He opened the door to let the room service waiter into the room.

While he ate the tasty boeuf bourguignon, he contemplated various plans. Any which way he mulled over the minutiae of the next stage of his scheme, he needed help. Other than the detective there was the Interpol agent Janssens, who made it clear he considered Nik and his grandfather neo-Nazi suspects. In effect, there was only one other person. Perhaps the detective believed him after overhearing his conversation with Konrad Resnik. Nik sighed and sat back in his chair, drinking a mouthful of Cabernet Franc from the Bordeaux region. Should he ring Detective Sauveterre? Would she listen and agree to his proposal to work together?

He snorted in frustration. What he knew of the detective from their interactions was her tenacity. She would not be easily swayed. He'd need a solid argument and evidence to convince her.

He padded into the bathroom, brushed his teeth and returned to the room, turning down the volume on the TV. He picked up the business card he had discarded on the desk, tapping it against the dark shiny table top. Nik dropped it back onto the desk, reached into his wallet and pulled out the detective's business card. He set it down next to the card Sébastien had given him, his attention flicking between both numbers.

With a sigh, he typed a phone number into his phone. It was time to find out who would help him.

CHAPTER 7

Iasos staggered in an attempt to dislodge the heavy hands from his shoulders, but they stayed firm and shoved him down onto a metal chair. The same bearlike paws wrenched his arms behind him and cable-tied his wrists, the thin plastic strip biting into his skin. The coarse black bag covering his head was yanked off. He blinked. Black spots dotted his vision. The luminescent artificial light rendered him sightless.

Iasos squinted, making out a shadowy form.

'Wh ...' He swallowed and coughed, his throat dry.

Someone uttered a few words. Iasos felt a plastic object pressed against his mouth and someone pulled his head back. Cool water touched his lips. Water dribbled down his chin and dampened his shirt as he gulped down the liquid. The bottle was taken away and his head released.

Iasos wheezed. He glared at the withered, wrinkled old man who stood before him. 'What do you want now, Pan Resnik? There was no need to bind me. Where can I go with this hulk of yours here to watch me?'

Resnik stared at him, his pale blue eyes as glacial as the ice caps in the Arctic Circle.

'I take it your meeting didn't go as expected,' Iasos commented.

'*Nie, nie dobre*. Your grandson led the police to the musée. Our negotiations were disrupted by a Detective Sauveterre, who shot Imrich.' The vein at Konrad's temple throbbed, his jaw tight. 'Most inconvenient. Imrich was a good, loyal soldier.'

Iasos went cold. 'What of my grandson, Nikolaos? Was he injured?'

'*Nie*. He managed to escape.' Resnik took a step towards Iasos. 'Your grandson is responsible for the death of my lieutenant.'

'Whatever he did, I'm sure it was in self-defence,' said Iasos.

'He aided the detective in the shooting, and for that he'll pay,' Resnik threatened. He flicked a glance at the beefy man standing behind Iasos, who wrenched Iasos's head back, neck stretched taut, his Adam's apple protruding. Iasos tried to swallow. His throat made a clicking sound.

'For decades, we've been searching for the lost coin of Herodotos,' Resnik continued. 'And the search is almost over. I shall use your grandson to locate the object. From what I have learned, you and he share an interest in the history of the ancient world, and he too has studied the classics.'

'I will kill you myself if you go anywhere near my grandson,' Iasos rasped.

Resnik waved a photo at him. 'Your wife was a beautiful woman. Was this a momentous occasion for you? An engagement perhaps?'

Iasos's chest rose and fell, the heat in his veins surging. 'I want my photo back.'

Resnik studied the photo. 'Such youthfulness and hope for the future in those joyous faces.' He then glared at Iasos. 'My family, stained with the wrongful accusations of my father's association with the Fuhrer, did not have the opportunity of happiness. My parents died as pariahs of society.'

Iasos blinked, unable to believe what Resnik was saying. 'How does that differ from you wanting to resurrect the Nazi regime to that of Hitler's plan?'

'The Fuhrer was plagued by paranoia and his egocentricity had lost sight of his original ambition for expanding the territory and to reunify the German people. I intend to reinstate his goal, and restore the rightful owners of our lands.'

'If Hitler could not succeed, what makes you believe you can?' asked Iasos.

Resnik smirked. 'Do not play the fool, Pan Zosimos. We both harbour Herodotos' coin, one of which I have and you have the other.'

'That's where you are wrong, I do not have such a coin.'

'No, but your grandson has the coin.' Resnik shoved the photo at Iasos. 'Technology has developed beyond all expectations. Today, altering pictures, even an old one like this, can be made to look like the original.' Resnik pointed at a Iasos's wife. 'A subtle adjustment where she stands and she disappears, in her place is your grandson waving the Nazi flag.' He clicked his fingers. 'He becomes the person of interest in a police hunt, wanted for questioning and alleged acts of terrorism.'

Iasos snorted. 'No-one would believe my grandson was involved in such activities.'

'Suspicion is more than enough to create doubt in the stoutest of officers.' Resnik's thin lips curved into a reptilian smile.

'You bastard!'

Iasos tried to wrestle free from his captor's heavy clutches. His head snapped back. He cursed at Resnik. His eyes widened as a fist as big as an anvil filled his vision and punched him in the nose. Blood projected from his nostrils and spittle flew from his mouth.

Blackness swam.

CHAPTER 8

Nik stood in the entryway of the bistro and scanned the few occupied tables. He raised a hand in greeting, and walked to the table.

'*Bonjour*, Sébastien,' said Nik, sliding into a chair opposite the Frenchman. 'Thank you for meeting me here so early.'

Sébastien set his coffee cup on the table. '*Pas de problème*, not a problem. I am happy to be here.'

'Would you like some breakfast?' asked Nik, catching the attention of a waiter.

Sébastien shook his head. '*Aucune pour moi*. I've eaten.'

'*Bonjour*, monsieur. Would you like to see a menu?' the waiter asked brandishing a glossy menu.

'*Bonjour*.' Nik nodded. '*Oui, merci*.' He glanced at the various options and then looked at Sébastien. 'What would you recommend?'

'I suggest the omelette with the ham and cheese. It is delicious and a good meal to start the day.'

'Sounds good, *merci*. May I also have a croissant and an

espresso?' Nik turned to his companion. 'Sébastien, are you sure you don't want something to eat?'

The taxi driver nodded. '*Je suis bonne, merci.*'

'Another coffee?'

'*Oui, merci,*' replied Sébastien.

The waiter nodded. '*Trés bon.*'

'*Merci beaucoup,*' said Nik.

When the waiter left them, Nik bit his lip, unsure what to say or where to begin. After all, the taxi driver was a stranger.

'Monsieur Nik, are you in trouble?' asked Sébastien, leaning forward, his brow furrowed.

Nik gave a sharp bark of laughter. 'It depends on how you define trouble.'

Sébastien beckoned him to lean closer and whispered, 'The police are searching for an Australian.'

Nik swallowed. 'Where did you hear that? Was it on the news? Radio?'

Sébastien shook his head. 'The police contacted my boss and requested all taxi drivers to report back to the police if they pick up an Australian.'

'There's a lot of Australians visiting Paris,' said Nik, a little optimistic.

'*Oui,* that is true, except they gave us your description.'

'Shit.'

'Why are the police after you?' Sébastien asked.

'I was to meet my grandfather—'

The waiter returned with the food and coffee.

'That looks delicious, *merci beaucoup,*' said Nik with an appreciative nod.

The waiter bowed. 'Enjoy your breakfast.' He moved on to another table.

'Where's your grandfather?'

'I don't know,' Nik replied. 'I was supposed to meet my

grandfather at the Hilton Paris Hotel, but he didn't show up. I reported him missing to the police and the following day I received a message to go to the Louvre. An Interpol agent met me at the museum, accusing my grandfather and me of being neo-Nazi terrorists and then explaining that my grandfather had disappeared in Marseilles.'

Sébastien's mouth fell open. '*Ce que le?* What?'

'I realise this sounds crazy. I wouldn't believe it myself if someone, a complete stranger, was telling me all this.' Nik studied the man who sat across from him. 'This is wrong. I shouldn't have called you.' Nik pushed his chair back.

'Monsieur Nik, I am here. I came regardless of the police notification. What has happened to your grandfather is terrible, and I want to help you if I can.'

Nik shook his head. 'I can't. It's too much to ask and why would you help me? You don't even know me.'

'I know good people when I meet them, and you are one. I can tell you care very much for your grandfather and family is important. Let me assist you,' said Sébastien.

Nik drew in a deep breath and exhaled. 'Okay. After the disturbing meeting with the Interpol agent I called the police again and met with Detective Sauveterre, who also thought we were involved with the neo-Nazis.' Nik clutched the cold steel of the fork. 'I'm hoping she has changed her mind after the shoot-out at the Musée Rodin.'

'That was you?' Sébastien's eyes grew wider.

'I didn't do the shooting but I was there. I had a visitor at the hotel who told me if I wanted to learn where my grandfather was, I had to meet a man called Konrad Resnik. I went to the museum to meet the person who abducted my grandfather, and Detective Sauveterre followed me. Things got messy when Resnik's bodyguard discovered her, and she tried to arrest them both.'

'Konrad Resnik? The shipping mogul?' asked Sébastien, his eyes as big as orbs.

Nik nodded and poked the fork into his omelette.

Sébastien sat back and whistled. 'My friend, you are in deep *merde*.'

'That, I know,' said Nik. 'I have a plan but I need your help to make it work. It's not dangerous, and I wouldn't ask if I knew anyone here.' He paused. 'Do you have a family? A wife and children?'

'*Oui*, and a girl and a boy.'

Nik shook his head. 'I can't ask you to do this.'

'Monsieur Nik, tell me what your plan is, and I'll decide if I can do what you ask or not,' said Sébastien.

'Can you drive me to Disneyland?'

Sébastien blinked. 'Disneyland? *Pourquoi?*'

'I'll explain.'

Nik outlined his idea, describing locations and scenarios if the arranged meeting with the detective did not work. He studied the Frenchman as a myriad of expressions flitted across his face. Nik poured water into a glass and took a drink. 'What do you think?'

Sébastien exhaled loudly through his nose. 'I think the idea is *fou*, crazy, but it may work, or you will be arrested. It will be better if I ask some friends to help out.'

'No,' said Nik, shaking his head. 'I don't want too many people getting involved. I didn't want to ask you to drive me, but I'm stuck, now more so with my identity circulating with your fellow drivers and possibly other public transport services.'

'I agree, your anonymity won't last, and your plan has a better chance of working the more people we have participating,' said Sébastien. 'My friends are discreet and know how to create a, how do you say *détournement* in English?'

Nik scratched his head. 'Do you mean diversion or distraction?'

'*Bon*, diversion!'

'I don't know, Sébastien. I don't want you or anyone else to get arrested on my behalf.'

Sébastien laughed and shrugged. '*Absurdité.* The police won't even know we are there.' He stood. 'Leave it to me, I will arrange. Tomorrow, midday at Disneyland, yes?'

Nik nodded. 'That is the time I said to Detective Sauveterre to meet me.'

'Best we leave at ten-thirty in the morning.'

'Okay. Thank you, Sébastien.'

'Of course, my friend. You are a visitor to my country and I'm sorry this has happened to your grandfather. We will make it right.' Nik gave him the name of his hotel and Sébastien tipped his head at him and departed.

Nik rose, put some money on the table and left the bistro. Time to pack his suitcase and be ready to move to another hotel after his meeting with the detective. He really needed somewhere to come and go without being tailed. Perhaps Sébastien may have some ideas where he could stay.

CHAPTER 9

The next morning, at ten-thirty sharp, Nik and Sébastien were on their way to Disneyland, the fun-themed park thirty-two kilometres south of Paris.

'Are you sure you want to go ahead with this meeting?' asked Sébastien in a dubious tone.

'No,' replied Nik, 'but there's only one way to find out if the detective accepts my proposition and whether she believes my grandfather and I are not Nazi sympathisers.' He patted his hip where he wore the concealed weapon. He had not intended to bring the pistol but at the last minute decided to do so. 'Thank you for driving me, Sébastien. I almost called you not to pick me up and instead take public transport.'

Sébastien stole a glance at him. 'That would have been unwise,' he said and turned his attention back to the road. 'The police have passed on your photo to bus and train drivers as well.'

'They are really trying to restrict my movements.' Nik voiced a few expletives and slumped in his seat. He stared out of the window as the outskirts of the city flashed by, discouraged by this latest news. 'Next they'll contact the hotels, and that will be the end of me, I've nowhere to go.'

'I can help you there. One of my friends has an Airbnb in Saint-Denis. I will ask him if the house is available and take you there after you have conducted your business with the detective,' said Sébastien.

Nik shook his head. 'I can't accept your gracious offer. I'll be putting you and your friend at risk with the police if they were to discover your involvement.'

Sébastien grinned. 'Monsieur Nik, my friends and I, how do you say *connaître la loi*, know the gendarme. When we were young and poor, to earn money we smuggled cigarettes into Germany, Belgium, Italy, Austria, Spain, Portugal, wherever we got good deals.'

'What made you stop?' asked Nik.

'I got married and the possibility I could be caught frightened my wife. One of my friends was arrested for smuggling in Italy, and spent ten years in jail. That's when I decided it was time to get a respectable job.'

'Seriously, Sébastien, I don't want you to get caught up in my mess and sent to prison for aiding me. You have a family to consider, and I don't want to be the person responsible for you being arrested.'

'This is different, and I want to help you find your grandfather. Besides, it's the right thing to do. And if the *flics* somehow learn that you were my fare, I know nothing other than driving you to a hotel.'

'You are a good man, Sébastien. And your friends too.' Nik bit his inner cheek and fell quiet seeing the signage for Disneyland and the distance remaining to reach the amusement park. As they sped along the motorway, more road signs displayed the decreasing kilometres as they got closer to Europe's famous playground.

'Will you deploy your friends around the park?' he asked, wanting to dispel the apprehension of his upcoming meeting with the detective.

'*Oui*. A few will remain outside the venue and others not too far from the building, a couple in a nearby store, while I and another friend will be inside the Disney studio with you.'

'Okay. The place should be busy and noisy enough to create a distraction if I have to escape.'

'And my friends will be ready to provide cover and guide you to the car park.'

'Let's hope it doesn't come to that.'

'Do you believe the detective will allow you to participate in the investigation?' Sébastien asked as they passed another large sign promoting Disneyland.

'She tried to arrest the man who's abducted my grandfather even though his enforcer held her at gunpoint.'

'She is a determined detective and one of France's top inspectors,' Sébastien warned.

'Good to know,' said Nik. 'Lucky for me she was distracted by the shooting incident, and I managed to avoid being detained.'

'*Excusez-moi?* And you arranged to meet with her? Monsieur Nik, I think you might be walking into a trap,' said Sébastien, concerned.

'I have considered that possibility but I need information on this man Resnik who has kidnapped my grandfather, and the only way to get it is through the police. Their database can locate any illegal connections and operations he's fronting.'

'Monsieur Nik, I know people who can access the information you want.'

'Let's first see how this meeting goes. If the detective doesn't agree to work with me, I'll take you up on your offer.' He rubbed his hands up and down his thighs, his mouth dry as they neared their destination. He wasn't sure how the detective would react to his proposal, but he had to try before exploring alternative avenues.

Thirty minutes later, they arrived at the large car park, already over half full of SUVs and sedans. Sébastien drove into a parking bay a few rows up from the bus port. Nik was about to get out of the car when Sébastien grabbed his arm.

'*Un* moment.' He took out his mobile. He spoke, paused to listen, and then ended the call. 'Everyone is here. They are waiting near the Disney Village. As soon as they see us, they'll move into position. My compatriots will call me when they see the police.'

'The officers know how to blend in with the crowd,' said Nik.

'Do not worry, my friends can spot them.'

'One day, you will have to tell me more about your former career,' said Nik, his brow raised.

Sébastien grinned and tapped his nose. 'I shall regale you with many stories.'

'I look forward to hearing them.' Nik got out of the car and gazed across the car park. He had no doubt the French constabulary were skilled at blending in with the public, but it was possible to detect the telltale signs when trained to discern the subtleties of being tailed. On his journey to Marseilles he had identified the two undercover officers Detective Sauveterre assigned to follow him, and then picked out the two new officers who replaced them. Given what Sébastien revealed, he and his friends were well versed in not only evading the officers but recognising them in a crowd.

'I'll wait here for ten minutes,' said Nik. 'That should be enough time for you to enter the studio before I do.'

'*Bonne chance*, good luck.'

'*Bonne chance* to you too,' said Nik.

Sébastien gave him a salute and sauntered away. Nik patted his pocket. At least he had the coin for a quick escape if the encounter went awry. After his phone call to the detective, he had destroyed the sim card, and bought another two. One he left in his luggage, which now sat in the boot of Sébastien's car, the other was in his mobile phone. He checked his watch and began his long walk to the theme park.

He followed the marque line and merged with families, side-stepping excited children who tried to break free from their parents' clutches, their eagerness to enter the amusement park topped with earnest pleas to run ahead. Nik began to doubt whether he had made the right decision in arranging to meet the detective. He scoured the faces around him, predicting the detective would have backup. It was a matter of what action she would take and how she deployed her officers.

At the end of the covered walkway, trees lined the path with patches of lawn framing the expansive, colourfully decorated pedestrian way. Nik slowed his pace to take in the sight. An enormous paved compass set into the walkway filled its centre. The site was bigger than he expected, with restaurants and cafés wherever he turned, and many shops, arcades and hotels, and movie studios. He could imagine how magical the amusement park would be at night, when it was illuminated.

Nik spied two undercover police officers taking selfies in front of the enormous statue of Mickey Mouse outside the World of Disney building. He walked past them, pretending to check the street signs of the park, and looked left and then right before ambling across the massive compass. He made his way to the Walt Disney Studios and waited in the queue to enter. Before long, he approached the attendant and purchased a ticket.

Nik skirted the water feature of a scene from Fantasia, where Mickey used magic on a broom to make it carry buckets of water. He bypassed the Walt Disney Studios store and headed for Studio 1, the location of his meeting with the detective. Families packed the studio, the atmosphere buzzed with excitement and high energy, notable by parents' indulgent smiles as they pointed out areas of interest to their children. A wide pathway ran through the centre marked with white painted lines to guide people, much like driving on a road, complete with pedestrian crossings running between store fronts. Wherever he turned, colourful fluorescent lights dazzled and heightened the enlivened atmosphere.

He entered the Legends of Hollywood store and stared. Merchandise in all forms from every Pixar, Star Wars and Disney film, stretched from one side of the shop to the other. There was a replica of the Volkswagen Beetle *Herbie*, jacked up on a car trolley in the Marvel section of the shop. Nik weaved in and out of the Star Wars collection and spotted Sébastien browsing the Marvel collection. He was picking out child-sized t-shirts from *The Incredibles* paraphernalia clothing rack.

Nik glanced around and wound his way towards a miniature Statue of Liberty.

'Detective Sauveterre, thank you for coming.'

The tall, attractive blonde woman turned to him, her tawny-coloured eyes appraised him. 'Monsieur Zosimos, your phone call and the invitation to meet surprised me. I didn't expect to see you so soon. I don't suppose you would come back with me to the police station for questioning?'

'Now why would I do that?' Nik scanned the store. 'How many police officers did you bring with you?'

'I am here alone.'

Nik regarded her. 'I've seen two outside by the restaurant, two more as I entered the studio gates, and I would say there are another two at the rear of this building. Why did you agree to meet me if you had no intention of listening to the information I have?'

She scowled at him. 'Monsieur Zosimos, I am a police officer. It would be remiss of me not to bring backup, and as you disappeared the last time we were together, I cannot allow that to happen again.'

'That is disappointing,' said Nik, his fingers tapping against his thigh. 'You are wasting time and resources on the wrong person. You should investigate Konrad Resnik, his ties with neo-Nazi and right-wing extremists. I wanted to collaborate with you rather than us being adversaries. You have made your position clear. *Au revoir*, detective.'

'It would be preferable if you came with me, where we can discuss your grandfather and Konrad Resnik,' she said, her eyes glinting.

Nik took a step back. 'I would rather not.'

'You must not communicate with Konrad Resnik again, Nikolaos,' she warned.

Nik's eyes widened at her use of his name.

'Monsieur Zosimos,' she corrected herself and pulled out her handcuffs. 'He is a highly regarded philanthropist with powerful and well-placed connections.'

Nik blinked. *Why would she tell me that?* 'I'll find my grandfather on my own if you don't intend to help me.'

She moved towards him, holding out the handcuffs. 'I cannot allow you to do that or leave until you are in my custody. It is for your own protection.'

Nik shook his head. 'No, that won't work for me.'

Quick as a cobra striking, he seized her hands and yanked her to him, trapping her hands against his chest. He kissed her. Her lips were soft and warm, and the scent of her perfume, a subtle heady lavender, sent butterflies fluttering in his stomach. He dragged his mouth away from hers, sidestepped around a pillar, and saw a familiar face moving towards him.

Janssens.

What the hell is he doing here?

With fast, long strides, Nik hastened through the store,

slipping on the black baseball cap with the words Eiffel Tower he had purchased days ago. Sébastien and several other men fell into step around him and surrounded him in a protective circle. There were shouts from behind them. Nik sped up and once outside, wove his way through the crowds amassed around the water feature.

'*Arrêt!* Stop!'

He zigzagged around prams, small children and parents.

'*Arrêtez cet homme!*'

Parents looked around startled, pulling their children closer. The shouts grew louder and closer.

'Monsieur Nik, I think it's time to run,' said Sébastien, tension in his voice.

'Keep walking and when I say go, you and your friends head towards the exit,' he said, as they hastened through the park.

'We can't leave you to the mercy of the police!' Sébastien glanced over his shoulder. 'They're getting close.'

Nik risked a look and saw Janssens and Detective Sauveterre weaving at a quick pace through the crowd, their officers swarming in from the left and right.

'I'll meet you at the car. Go now!' Nik veered left, joined the rear of a group of tourists and then broke away heading for a cluster of trees.

He glanced over his shoulder and saw Janssens call out and point to Sébastien and his friends. He swung away just as Detective Sauveterre began to turn in his direction, and the undercover officers converged and began to follow them. The men split up and headed in different directions, blending in with the crowd. Nik half walked and half ran towards the trees. He hoped Sébastien and his friends were able to shake off their pursuers.

Nik reached into his pocket as he emerged from the shade of the trees and sped towards a larger and denser group of trees that formed part of the Fantasia Gardens. He stepped into the shadows, where he was hidden from the path and the view of passers-by. Nik looked around to make sure no-one had followed him or could see him.

He took out the coin and flipped it into the air. As the coin spun, he gritted his teeth.

Nik landed in the car park on his hands and knees, heaving, the sound of the pounding of feet drawing closer.

'*Mon dieu!* Monsieur Nik, are you alright?'

Nik nodded and gulped, unable to speak.

'You must have run very fast,' Sébastien said, hands on hips and puffing, his cheeks ruddy.

Nik sagged onto his haunches his head tilted back as he drew in ragged breaths. 'Fast ... is one ... word for it.'

Sébastien dangled a bottle of water in front of him.

'*Merci.*' Nik took a swig of water when his breathing steadied. 'I think it's time to leave.'

They were soon in the car and driving to Paris. Nik leaned his head back against the car seat and closed his eyes. His mind kept returning to the kiss with the detective and how soft her lips were, the smell of lavender on her skin and how she responded. His heart did a flip. He had surprised himself and her with the impromptu embrace, and when he broke off the kiss, her cheeks had a rosy tint to them. He rubbed his brow and redirected his thoughts to the presence of the Interpol agent.

The only logical reason for Janssens being there was that he and the detective were working together. He felt disappointed once again at being duped by the detective. He had been surprised to see the agent and hadn't considered the possibility Janssens would be there. Not when the arrangement was between him and the detective. He cursed under his breath. A naïve, rookie's mistake. He would not be deceived again.

Sébastien's voice interrupted his revery.

'That was quite the diversion, Monsieur Nik,' he said in admiration. 'It did the trick, although you almost got caught. The encounter did not go as you had planned? What happened?'

Nik opened his eyes and adjusted his cap. 'She was there to arrest me.'

'*C'est de la merde.*'

Nik sighed. 'You said it, Sébastien. That is shitty, but she's doing her job. My fault for pinning too much hope on what happened at the Musée Rodin and that she would agree to work with me. I was wrong.' He sat up. 'You mentioned you have an acquaintance who can find the information I'm after?'

Sébastien nodded. '*Oui.* She is, what you would call a hacker, and exceptionally good at uncovering information from anywhere in the world.'

'I'm so sorry.'

'*Quoi? Pourquoi?*'

'For putting you and your friends at risk with the law enforcement.'

The Frenchman grinned. 'Don't worry about us, we know how to avoid being captured.'

Nik bit his lip. 'I'm not sure if I should be happy that you do, but I am.'

Sébastien chuckled and they fell into companionable silence until they neared the outskirts of Paris. The traffic increased as they drove past the high-rise buildings in the Nanterre district.

'We've come back via a different route,' Nik commented.

'*Oui.* I'm taking you to see my friend.'

CHAPTER 10

Sébastien drove along a quiet street where across from a block of apartment buildings was a park. The squeals and shouts of the children playing football filtered through Nik's window. A group of parents sat on benches chatting. The air of normalcy contrasted with his dark mood after his narrow escape from the detective and Janssens.

'Wait in the car until I return,' said Sébastien. 'There are surveillance cameras in the street.'

Nik watched Sébastien cross the street and approach a cream-coloured stone apartment building with a sloping four-sided mansard roof. He pressed a buzzer by the tall, gated entrance, glanced over his shoulder and gave Nik the thumbs up. The gate opened and Sébastien stepped through it.

Nik tilted the bill of his cap lower and peered out the windscreen, his knee bouncing up and down. Why did the detective mention the Slovakian had friends in positions of power? Was it a slip of the tongue or was it a warning? Was she trying to give him a hint? Or was it a lie, just like the trap she orchestrated to capture him? He pursed his lips and blew air out of his nostrils, his thoughts wandering back to their brief embrace. It was spontaneous, the only thing he could think of to distract her from cuffing him. And it had worked. What he had not expected was the exhilaration of their kiss.

He recalled the jolt of electricity when they shook hands, even their initial eye contact ignited an unexpected reaction when they had first met at the hotel. These were emotions he had not experienced before, and it was as if he were in a rudderless boat, under the control of volatile currents. This was not the time to get distracted by a beautiful woman, and not by one who fooled him. If she had given him time to explain his plan, he would not need to resort to subterfuge and using unconventional methods to find his grandfather.

Sébastien yanked the car door open. 'Monsieur Nik! I have arranged to introduce you to my friend, but we must be quick. She has diverted the feed from the cameras on the street.'

Nik got out of the car, and they hurried across the road to the unlocked gate. Sébastien led Nik through the marble archway, an elaborate entrance where horse-drawn carriages would have been driven through in the nineteenth century. Doric columns with stone plinths topped with ornate brass vases masquerading as lamps were interspersed throughout the entrance way. They stepped into a wrought-iron elevator that took them to the fifth floor.

Sébastien led Nik along the sunlit passageway. Opposite two windows that faced onto the street were two larger-than-normal doors painted in black, creating a stark contrast against the white walls and ceiling. A door painted in bright blue was at the end of the corridor. Sébastien halted and pressed the doorbell. A petite and pretty, dark-haired woman in her forties opened the door. She gazed at Nik and looked him up and down.

'This is ridiculous. I don't have time for this.' He wheeled around.

'Monsieur Nik, wait!' said Sébastien. He spoke to the woman in French, the words clipped and terse. She retorted and ended the conversation with a haughty sniff.

'Sébastien, let's go. Your friend doesn't intend to help.' Nik gave her a disdainful glare and said, 'Why did you bother to admit us into the building if you weren't going to help me?'

'I wanted to see for myself the foreigner the police are searching for and has eluded capture,' she replied. 'Sébastien says you are a schoolteacher.'

'I am.'

She snorted. 'A schoolteacher who escapes not once but twice from France's most successful and experienced detectives. Who are you really?'

'A tourist who came to see the historic sites of France with his grandfather, and whose grandfather has been kidnapped by Konrad Resnik.'

'Konrad Resnik? You are involved with the industrialist?'

'Now I am,' replied Nik with a curt nod. 'I must find my grandfather, and in order to locate his whereabouts I need every piece of information on Resnik.'

She stepped aside. '*Entrer.*'

Nik glanced at Sébastien, who gave a slight shrug as they stepped into the apartment.

'What material do you require?' she asked.

'Whatever you can find on Resnik, from his birth, his life, how he became one of Europe's richest industrialists. Any past connections to the Nazi regime and Hitler, and present allegiances and notable alliances, including those who hold government positions,' he answered, checking each point off on his fingers.

'You believe Resnik has government officials on his payroll?' asked Sébastien, his forehead creased.

'A man like Resnik doesn't get to his position of wealth and power without some inside support from one or two bureaucrats, and those who can cover up his illicit enterprises.' He paused. 'The detective let it slip that Resnik has contacts within the ministry and possibly the constabulary.'

'Pardon? Are you sure the detective said that?' the woman asked, astonished. 'She wasn't feeding you a line?'

Nik grimaced. 'I can't be sure, not after she tried to arrest me, but it did sound like a hint.'

'That is out of character for Detective Sauveterre. Why do you suppose she gave you a clue?' she asked, narrowing her eyes.

He shook his head. 'I've been trying to work that out since we left Disneyland.'

'What I would like to know is how did you manage to evade capture from France's coldest and most relentless detective on the force?' The hacker crossed her arms against her chest.

'He disarmed her with a passionate kiss,' Sébastien chortled, patting Nik on the shoulder. 'It was *fantastique*. The detective was about to handcuff Monsieur Nik when he caught her off guard. He slipped away as quickly as he had embraced her with a kiss.'

The hacker's mouth gaped. '*Pas du tout!*'

'I don't think she'll fall for the same trick twice,' Nik said in a mild tone.

'*Pas de*, no. She'll be more determined to catch you now.' The hacker appraised him with interest.

Nik growled. 'Then the sooner I get the information and find my grandfather, the quicker we return to Australia and leave this unpleasant state of affairs and unmitigated fiasco behind us. How long will it take you to gather what you can on Resnik?'

'It depends on the firewalls. Some material will be easy to access, the more obscure Intel, such as his connections, will take time and require finesse.' She paused. 'There is the possibility I won't find anything. Resnik and his ilk are pre-computers, his life and background may not be online.'

'There will be some information, even on the dark web,' Nik pointed out.

She agreed. '*Oui*, it will take me a few hours.'

Sébastien clapped his hands. 'I shall leave you in Odette's capable hands, Monsieur Nik. I've my shift to cover and will return when I have finished.'

'Wait—'

'You'll be safe here.'

Nik glanced at unsmiling Odette and sighed. 'Fine, I guess.'

Sébastien patted him on the shoulder, and then spoke to Odette in French. She rolled her eyes and gave a one-word response. The Frenchman smiled at Nik and departed.

CHAPTER 11

Nik looked around the apartment. The parquetry had seen better days but was clean. The kitchen had been remodelled with seamless lines and had fresh twenty-first century fittings. The white cupboards and paint contrasted with the charcoal settee and graphite-coloured round dinner table and upholstered chairs. Opposite the dining table was a balcony that opened out onto the street and overlooked the park. Nik could hear the muffled yells and laughter of the children through the glass door. He glanced at a laptop on the coffee table in front of the settee.

'Where is the rest of your equipment?' he asked.

Odette went into the kitchen and pulled out a French press coffee pot and two small cups from an overhead cupboard. 'What do you mean?'

'The laptop is not your only digital device, and we should get started.'

She filled the pot with water and spooned coffee granules into the funnel. 'We've plenty of time. Sébastien won't be back for hours. He'll first go home to his family before returning.'

'Maybe so, but my grandfather doesn't have the luxury of time. We can start looking into Resnik's life and those he has on his payroll. The results may lead to other avenues of Intel I can use.'

She ignited the gas stove and set down the kettle to boil. 'Resnik is a very private man. He spent his youth building his father's wealth and creating further riches, both legally and illegally, and has ensured he's untouchable.'

Nik leaned against the wall and eyeballed her. 'How do you know that about him?'

Odette glanced at him. 'I came across Konrad Resnik when doing a bit of recon on how to break into the top ten industrialists' computer operating and security systems.'

'What did you learn about him?' he asked, levering himself away from the wall.

'What I've told you.'

He probed her brown eyes. 'There's more, tell me.'

The kettle gurgled and she poured the hot water into the pot. Soon the scent of coffee percolating filled Nik's nostrils.

'There has been chatter he had orchestrated the assassinations of high-ranking officials who opposed him, but no proof to charge him. It appears he was out of the country at the time of their mysterious deaths and seen in the company of other people. With these strong alibis and no evidence to tie him to the murders, he can continue with his businesses as normal.'

'What you found further confirms what the detective implied, that he has stooges in the government and police force.'

'He is a dangerous man,' she warned as she turned away from the stove.

'I know,' said Nik. He watched her pour the black brew into the cups. 'That's why any documentation or reports you find are essential. The more leverage I have, the better chance I have in rescuing my grandfather and stopping Resnik.'

She passed him a cup. 'Why does he have your grandfather? This is not his usual method of operating.'

'It's a misunderstanding,' replied Nik. 'Resnik mistook my grandfather for someone he isn't.'

She stared at him. 'I don't believe you are telling me the whole truth, but Sébastien is a good friend, and he has vouched for you. I'll see what I can uncover on Resnik.' She tossed back the coffee in one gulp, placed her cup in the sink and rubbed her hands together. 'To work.' She scurried over to the lounge and sat at her laptop, her fingers flying over the keyboard like a ballet dancer pirouetting on stage.

Nik scratched his head. 'Seriously, where are your computers and network?'

'You've watched too many spy shows,' she answered, her attention focused on her screen. 'My laptop is powerful enough for your request, and besides, it's not the machine, it's the person who uses it.'

'Ah-huh ... I have a feeling you are holding back on me,' he said, setting his empty cup in the sink.

'Just as you are not being honest with me.' She pointed to the screen. 'I can make an educated guess from the search terms you gave me.'

Nik stood by the balcony door and gazed out over the park, watching the children running and playing football. 'Best you don't, for your safety and Sébastien's.' He rubbed his brow and stared at his reflection in the glass.

'Is this why you wanted to talk to the detective? To request the information from her?' asked Odette.

He turned around. 'That was the intention. I was being a bit too optimistic and trusting in assuming Detective Sauveterre would assist me. I thought she would believe me and agree to our working together after the confrontation with Resnik and his bodyguard.' He shrugged. 'Now I know otherwise, and I will use whatever means and resources necessary to discover what Resnik's motivation is, and where he is holding my grandfather.'

She arched a brow at him, the silence between them stretching. Nik shoved his hands into the pockets of his jacket and stared back at her. It was as if she were dissecting him like a rat in a science experiment.

She patted the seat next to her. 'Come, sit,' she said, and turned her attention back to the laptop.

Nik frowned. The glow from the screen gave her face a neon white pallor and made her hair appear darker. He felt he had passed a test of sorts. He sat next to her and glanced at the screen, the background black, the typeset white. The display reminded him of old photos he'd seen of the first personal computers with a MS-DOS operating system where the cursor flashed in either green or grey and there was only the font. No pictures, ads, or pop-ups to distract the end user.

He sat silent, watching as her fingers typed a series of commands. The minutes dragged by, Nik drummed his fingers on the armrest, his foot tapping.

'Have you found anything much?' he asked her after thirty minutes had passed.

'The usual stuff: where and when he was born, the name of his parents, the names of his siblings, wife and children. Where he grew up and went to school. Nothing out of the ordinary.'

'Can you include in your search parameters connections with Hitler or Himmler and Ahnenerbe?'

'Ahnenerbe? Who are they?'

'Himmler created a secret organisation,' Nik answered, 'with the primary aim to prove that Germans were descended from a god-like race and validating the Third Reich's vision of an Aryan race.'

'*Mon dieu*, they were monsters,' she said, disgusted. 'Let's see what we can find.'

Odette typed in the terms and the search engine came back with fifty links. They skimmed the headings and the abstract.

'That one,' he pointed. 'And that one too.'

Odette clicked on the first link. Nik leaned a little closer, elbows on his knees and scanned through the content.

'Holy shit,' he breathed. 'He was in Hitler's Young People's program. That explains a few things.'

'He wasn't old enough to be a member of the group,' said Odette. 'The war ended in 1945, which means if he was involved in Hitler's Youth, it was only for two years.'

Nik disagreed. 'That was not the only initiative Hitler implemented. From the age of ten, all German boys joined *Jungvolk*, the Young People's group, and when they turned fourteen, they graduated to Hitler's Youth. The girls had a similar program. Their objective was to educate German children and teenagers in the Third Reich's ideology so when they became adults, they would continue Hitler's skewed philosophy.'

'How do you know about these projects of Hitler's?' she asked.

'As I mentioned earlier, I'm a teacher. I teach history, I specialise in ancient history but also teach modern history. Two years is enough to indoctrinate a child whose mind is malleable enough to believe the lies taught to them. Is there more on Resnik's early life and that of his parents'? They must have been Nazi supporters for Resnik to be enrolled in the Young People's group. And what of his siblings? Where are they now? Did they also enlist?'

'We shall find out.' Odette was about to type a new search command when Nik stopped her.

'Wait, can we see that other website, the one on the Aryan race?'

She scrolled further down and clicked on the link. They read the text in silence. Nik slumped back and stared at the screen.

'*Mon dieu!*' Odette's eyes widened.

'I want to know more about his parents and his childhood,' said Nik in a quiet voice.

Odette's fingers beat out a quick staccato on the keyboard. 'He's resumed Hitler's plan and recruited millions of people from around the world. What is this secret weapon he is talking about? From the speech Resnik presented, Hitler was also searching for it and if he had found it, he would have won the war. Resnik claims he possesses one half of the object and is seeking the other. Do you know what he's looking for?'

'I may,' replied Nik. 'There may be some event that occurred in his childhood or adolescence that triggered his quest to re-imagine Hitler's vision.'

'Such as?'

'Could be anything. A trauma, or he witnessed an incident that strengthened his belief in the regime.'

'Strengthened his belief?' Odette glanced at him, her forehead crinkled.

'Let's presume he was a devout Nazi follower and in his mind a soldier in Hitler's army. Whatever happened to him as a child would have further substantiated his view of Hitler's ideals and led him to adopt them as his own.'

'You got that from reading the article?' she asked.

'It's psychology, but what I require is more information to corroborate his intentions.'

'*Oui*, let's see what else we can find.'

'I need to know who he has on his payroll. You must have a way to infiltrate his bank accounts.'

She grinned. '*Oui*. The means and many ways.'

CHAPTER 12

'**D**o you have a spare memory stick to upload the articles?' Nik asked Odette some hours later.

'*Pourquoi?*'

'To review the contents and use as leverage against the people Resnik has paid off,' he replied standing up, stretching his back, and rotating from side to side.

'That is unwise and dangerous,' Odette said, her brows furrowed. 'Having this material alone on the Prime Minister is enough to get you killed.'

'I know,' he said, lowering himself back onto the couch. 'But if it gets me my grandfather back, it's worth the risk.' He gave her a crooked smile. 'Besides, what sort of threat am I, a mere high school teacher?'

'If you are sure.' She gave him a hard look.

He met her gaze. 'I am.'

Odette stood. 'I will get a memory stick to save those sources.' When she returned, she waved her mobile at Nik. 'Sébastien just messaged, he'll be here around 6 pm.'

A few hours later there was a knock at the door. Odette got up to admit Sébastien. He entered the apartment with a cheery greeting and a spring in his step.

'Did Odette find the information you wanted, Monsieur Nik?' he asked, looking at the hacker who was grinning like a cat that caught the proverbial mouse.

'*Oui*,' she responded. 'I have, as they say in English, "come through with the goods".'

'She has indeed,' said Nik, rising. He turned to the petite woman. 'Thank you for uncovering the Intel on Resnik, Odette. I am indebted to you. If you decide to visit Australia, make sure you let me know and I will show you around.'

She shrugged. '*Tout cela en une journée de travail.*' Odette's face became serious. 'You must tread carefully, Teacher. These men are not easily intimidated, and they will not react well to threats.'

'My desire is not to use the information against them, but it's good leverage if I ever need it. My plan to get the detective on-side didn't work, so I must change tack and find other ways to rescue my grandfather.'

Odette bit her lip. 'I am sorry this has happened to your grandfather, and if you require further information or help in any other way, you can contact me through Sébastien.'

Nik smiled at her. 'Thank you very much. I hope this is the extent of our exchange.' He stood next to Sébastien. 'Can you disable the surveillance cameras again for us to leave?'

'*Bien sûr.*'

'A slight problem,' said Sébastien shaking his head. 'Our taxi company received further notifications that if we pick you up as a fare, we are to call the police right away.'

'That is just great,' said Nik, running his fingers through his hair.

Odette typed into her laptop. 'It appears the taxi companies are not the only ones the police department have contacted.' She turned the screen towards Nik. 'Train, airport and Uber drivers, hotels and motels.'

'Damn! They are hemming me in.'

'I suggest you stay here for now,' Sébastien said. 'It would be unwise to travel while they publicise your photo.'

Odette shook her head and spoke to Sébastien in French. The taxi driver's eyes flicked towards Nik before responding. Odette crossed her arms and narrowed her eyes, and sniffed, her nose scrunched.

'Look, I don't want to cause any problems. Besides, what about your friend with the Airbnb? I thought that was all arranged?' asked Nik, trying to keep calm.

'I suggest you stay here a few days for the time being.' Sébastien held up his hand as Nik began to protest. 'Only until the situation becomes less risky for you.' He cut a sharp gaze at the hacker. 'In the meantime, Odette will make you comfortable.'

Odette pursed her lips. '*Ma maison est ta maison.* You will be my special guest.'

'Thank you, Odette, but I do not want to burden you or impose on your hospitality any further.' Nik looked at Sébastien. 'There must be a way to avoid being identified?'

The Frenchman frowned. 'Not right now. There are cameras on every street. Best to wait a few days, and then I'll take you to my friend's house.'

'Odette disabled the camera on our arrival, can you do the same for the journey to the house?' Nik asked her.

'*Oui,* if I had the address.'

Nik raised his brows at Sébastien. 'Well?'

'I understand your frustration, Monsieur Nik. It is safer for you to remain out of sight for a few days at least.' He patted Nik on the shoulder. 'I'll get your suitcase from my car.'

CHAPTER 13

Nik emerged from the spare bedroom and went into the kitchen.

'That coffee smells good,' he said. 'Can I help?'

'You can carry the plate of almond turnovers,' Odette replied.

Nik picked up the platter and followed Odette to the settee, setting the plate on the coffee table. He then checked his phone for messages, turned it off and set it next to the plate.

He gazed at Odette as she poured the coffee. 'Don't you have a job to go to? I've been here for a couple of days, and you haven't been out except to buy pastries and food,' he asked.

'I was once a financial broker, but after my parents passed away, I didn't need to work anymore. I own several apartments in this building,' she replied.

'Right. So why do you hack?'

She shrugged. 'The challenge of besting complex firewalls keeps my brain active, and it's fun. Why did you become a teacher?'

'To provide students with skills to become independent learners and develop a love of learning. My best experiences are from working with students from low socioeconomic areas. Their hardships and lack of stability at home have taught me to be a better teacher and someone they can trust.'

'You enjoy being a teacher.'

'Teaching students is the best part of the job, not the mountain of marking and paperwork, nor the negative publicity and blame when something goes wrong. The wider community expects much more from educators today, including the role of parenting, which is not why I became a teacher.'

'So why keep doing it?'

'A good question. I am considering a move into research like my grandfather did, and work in a university.'

'You could work here, at one of our universities,' she said, 'and live in Paris.'

'That is an appealing suggestion.' He gave her a half smile. 'When you go out next, are you able to purchase SIM cards for my mobile?'

'*Oui*,' Odette nodded. 'I can change the number for you on the SIM card.'

'I didn't think that was possible. I thought only the service provider can alter the phone number.'

'*Oui*, that is so. But I can access the service provider's operating system to create a new number for you.'

Nik whistled, impressed. 'Is there any computer mainframe you cannot get into?'

Odette paused for a few seconds. '*Non*.'

'That will work in the interim, but I will still need replacement SIM cards for when I leave here.' He clenched a hand. 'I really must resume searching for my grandfather using the information you found for me.'

'I understand how exasperating this waiting and not being able to do anything is for you,' she said. 'I can dig deeper if you tell me a bit more about why Resnik kidnapped your grandfather.'

Nik gazed across the park and the historic rooftops, a distinctive feature of the Paris skyline. 'No,' he said, shaking his head. 'You are involved more than I wanted.'

'You planned to work with the detective,' she pointed out. 'I can assist you more with the research than she can ever find on the police database and network.'

He turned to her. 'I have no doubt you can. She is trained to deal with dangerous situations and she's the lead detective assigned to find my grandfather. I would not be here if she agreed to work with me.'

She tilted her head at him with a knowing smirk.

'What?' he asked.

'Are you in love with the detective?' she asked.

'I ... what? No.'

'Are you sure? It sounds as if you are when you talk about her.'

'I admire her tenaciousness and how driven she is to do her job, no matter how misguided she is regarding who is the guilty party,' he answered. 'That's all.'

'Perhaps her intentions were to bring you into protective custody to prevent Resnik from abducting you too. Who knows what he will do if he seizes you.'

Nik snorted. 'That's not what I believe she intimated, not from our brief conversation. As to Resnik, I'm not much of a threat to him or his operation. He wants something I cannot give.'

'The object he seeks?' she asked.

He nodded. 'Which is why I must track down these leads, no matter the risk of being caught by the police.'

'When the National Police search for dangerous felons, they call in the Gendarmerie and the Municipal Police to assist. I have not seen any evidence of this on the police threads.' She regarded him, her gaze fierce.

'It's a good thing I'm not dangerous or a criminal.'

'I will get your SIM cards.'

CHAPTER 14

Nik used his laptop to scroll through the information Odette had uncovered, checking over his notations on Resnik's associates and their locations. There wasn't much he had missed from his previous readings and analysis. What he needed to do was journey to those places and see where they led him. Odette continued to search for more details on Resnik and his collaborators, going back to the family's connection with the Nazi Party and tracing potential results to the catalyst behind the industrialist's desire to fulfil Hitler's ideals.

Odette's mobile rang. She talked for a few minutes and hung up. She resumed typing on her laptop.

'Sébastien is coming today.'

'Okay, that's good,' Nik said, relieved. He could finally use the Intel to track his grandfather's whereabouts.

He concentrated on the list of cities frequented by Resnik, and the connection to his place of residence, a castle on the outskirts of Zilina. He studied the aerial shot, the impenetrable forest on the mountain slopes of Král'ova Hol'a, the perfect shield and natural defensive perimeter. The castle was remote and far enough away to avoid drop-ins by authorities or anyone inquisitive. Nik surmised his grandfather was held captive there, but without evidence to support his theory, it was an educated guess. He needed proof, and how to get it was the issue. He opened another file and saw Odette had uploaded recent photos of Resnik with various associates. Nik clicked on the latest photo and zoomed in on the man next to Resnik.

Odette closed her laptop and went to the fridge. She pulled out a bottle of champagne and grabbed two flutes from a cupboard. She walked back to where Nik sat on the sofa, removed the foil and popped the cork and handed him a glass.

'What are we celebrating?' he asked.

'New friendships and to rescuing your grandfather,' she replied as she sat down next to him.

'I'll drink to that.' He raised his glass to her. 'Thank you for everything you've done for me, your hospitality and your friendship.'

'*C'est un honneur.*'

He downed a mouthful of the chilled sparkling wine.

'Who's that man with Resnik?' She pointed.

'I am guessing he is Resnik's new bodyguard,' he replied.

'He's big and evil-looking.' She bit her lip. 'You will be careful, Nik.'

'I will do my best to keep out of trouble,' he said and gave her a smile of reassurance.

Her brow wrinkled. 'He appears to be a man who doesn't have any qualms about killing.'

'I can look after myself, Odette.' He glanced back at the photo. 'I know how to fight.'

Nik was zipping up his suitcase when Odette appeared outside the bedroom. She loitered around the doorway, sending him furtive looks. He glanced over his shoulder at her and slipped his laptop into his backpack.

'Odette, is there something the matter?'

She thrust a black plastic card at him and a mobile phone. 'I want you to take these.'

He stared at her. 'You have done so much for me, I can't—'

She stepped into the room and held out the card. 'The card is untraceable. There is enough money on it to avoid you having to use your credit card and being tracked by the police. I'll add money when you need it.'

'Odette—'

'Use this phone to contact me.' She continued as if he hadn't spoken. 'Call me when you are travelling, and I'll divert the surveillance cameras and shut down access to airports, train and bus ports where there are CCTV.' She held the items out. Nik took them from her and enveloped her in his arms. 'Don't you get killed.' She muttered into his ear.

Nik smiled. 'I have no intention of doing that.'

'I best disable the street cameras. Sébastien will be here any moment.'

'Right. I'm almost done.'

Nik checked the room to be sure he had packed all his belongings. He grabbed his suitcase and backpack, and went into the living room. He set his bags down by the sofa, put the phone Odette had given him into his backpack and slipped the card into his wallet.

He rested his hands on his hips and shifted his thoughts to his next move. Careful preparation was required, otherwise he would never rescue his grandfather. Odette's comment about Resnik's new bodyguard was an astute observation. While he hadn't tested his fighting skills other than sparring with his trainer or used any of the weapons his grandfather had drilled him in, Nik was confident he could protect himself and inflict serious injury on his opponent.

Nik patted the concealed gun under his jacket and felt the weight of the dagger strapped to his leg. *Who would have thought that I, a high school history teacher, would be carrying weapons and searching for his grandfather in a conspiracy about a magical coin?*

He sat down on the sofa, elbows on his knees, head lowered. Since he had arrived in Paris, he'd never experienced such loneliness or despondency as he did at this moment. He had spent the first week in conversations with the police and Interpol, and gone to Marseilles to visit the antiquities store, the last place his grandfather was seen. His heart constricted as if someone had squeezed it as he recalled the conversations with his parents and contacting the school to extend his leave. In these past few days he had grappled with being unable to search for his grandfather, but at least he now had good Intel on Resnik, his family and contacts. He rubbed his forehead.

There was a knock at the door. Odette let Sébastien in.

'Odette, I don't know how I'm going to repay you for what you have done,' said Nik.

She waved a hand. 'I'm glad I could help and that you find your grandfather.'

He nodded and kissed her on the cheek. '*Merci beaucoup, mademoiselle.*'

Sébastien held out a piece of paper. 'Odette, this is the direction I'm driving. Can you please divert the cameras along the way?'

She smiled at Nik. '*Au revoir,* and good luck.'

CHAPTER 15

Nik gazed out the window at the changing street scape as Sébastien drove through the outskirts of Paris and towards Saint-Denis. The industrial area had new buildings, concrete and glass edifices, contrasting against the charm of the older nineteenth-century apartments. He rubbed his hand over his jeans pocket where the coin sat, a seemingly innocuous object with a historic legacy that defied the laws of physics. He remembered the day his grandfather showed him the coin and shared a little of its history. When he agreed to be the coin's next guardian, his grandfather had disclosed the whole truth of their family's association and legacy with the unusual heirloom.

At first he didn't believe his grandfather, until he did a bit of research himself. Papou showed him the secret bunker under his house, fitted out with the latest computers and software, and a surveillance system that rivalled the likes of ASIO, Ministry of State Security in China, Interpol, MI5, CIA and other country's secret service organisations. Then there was the museum section of the bunker, weapons from antiquity dating back to the Battle of

Thermopylae to sophisticated modern-day weaponry and armoury. And the extraordinary collection of rare books that included first editions of the *Iliad* and the *Odyssey*.

He had thought the coin was unique but it had a sibling, both fashioned from a stone once owned by Herakles, the first person to learn the truth of the stone. The legendary hero from Greek mythology kept the properties of the stone a secret. An ancestor of Helen of Sparta moved to Aegina with his family and smelted the stone into the two coins. The mystery of the coins' power remained until an alchemist, who was also a guardian, experimented with the coin and discovered how to use it. There was no evidence if the guardian experienced any side effects from using the coin, except subsequent protectors of the precious object never revealed its secret, and over the centuries the knowledge of how to harness its power was long forgotten. That was until Nik took a chance and used it to travel back to Perth to buy a new mobile phone and arm himself with weapons from his grandfather's bunker.

'Did Odette find the information you required?' Sébastien asked, disrupting his thoughts.

'She did,' Nik replied. 'Thank you for introducing me to her. Though I don't think she was too keen in having an uninvited house guest, not that she said as such.'

'She is, how do you say, puts on a façade and *barrières*, does not show her true self. Odette is *au cœur tendre,* soft-hearted in spite of her gruff manner.'

'She is a very good hacker. I would not have been able to find the information she managed to extract about Resnik from the dark web. I hope Odette doesn't mind if I reach out to her if I need further research or to clarify some of the searches she did for me.'

'I don't think that will be a problem. You must have changed her mind somehow during your stay with her. Odette's difficult to impress and doesn't let herself get attached to people.' Sébastien paused for a moment. 'The detective who is pursuing you, are you attracted to her?'

Nik snorted. 'She is hunting me, not quite the seductive approach to getting to know someone.'

'But you—'

'But nothing,' he said, his brow knitted. 'The detective is doing her job and I'll do whatever it takes to save my grandfather.'

They fell silent. Nik's left temple throbbed, and he pressed a hand against his head to ease the pressure. He did not need a headache, not with so much to do.

'What if you don't come back?' asked Sébastien after a few moments.

'I'll return and with my grandfather.' He squeezed his eyes shut, the pain spreading across his forehead. 'How much farther is it to your friend's place?'

'We've arrived.' Sébastien came to a stop outside a house, the street short and with a few houses that backed onto a park. Trees bordered the residences and made the street seem secluded, with the one road in and out.

'Your friend rents out this house?' Nik asked, staring at the unassuming two-storey brick house with a pretty garden.

'*Oui.* He and his family live in Normandy and use the house when they come to Paris. He leases it to tourists most of the year.' They got out of the car and Nik looked around his new surroundings. The street was quiet, and people who resided there appeared to be well-to-do, judging from the Audis, BMWs, Mercedes and Maseratis, including one Tesla parked on the street.

Nik trailed behind Sébastien on a gravel path across the well-kept lawn, the way lined with low shrubs. In the flower beds under the window and to the left of the front door were lavender plants, their fragrance perfuming the air. A white picket fence bordered the front yards between the neighbouring properties.

They stepped through the door onto a small landing and Sébastien led him into the living room. Sunlight from the floor to ceiling windows flooded the cosy, comfortable space. Outside, a tall hedge created a fence between the properties and ran along the rear of the yard. Beyond that Nik could see oak trees in the park, clustered together to form a dense arbour.

The décor was modern and elegant, with white-washed walls and red kitchen appliances to contrast with the stark palette. The sofa was white suede with aqua, cerulean and light green cushions, and a grey angora blanket draped over the armrest.

'This is too generous,' he said to Sébastien. 'I can't stay here. Your friend must have tourists wanting to lease the place.'

Sébastien waved a hand as if to shoo a fly. 'My friend heard about your grandfather on the news and when I asked if you could stay, he said the house was yours for as long as you need.'

'I must pay a letting fee for my time here.'

Sébastien's coffee-coloured locks shook from side to side and he frowned at him. '*Vous ne!* You need not worry about payment, focus on saving your grandfather.' He beckoned Nik into the kitchen and opened the pantry. 'I have filled the cupboard with food and stocked the fridge.' He took out a couple of bottles of beer from the fridge and handed one to Nik.

'*Merci beaucoup.*' Nik said as he unscrewed the cap. He raised the bottle to his new-found friend. 'Cheers.'

Sébastien grinned. 'Cheers, mate.'

Nik laughed and drank a mouthful of the Kronenbourg. 'Thank you. I don't know how I can repay you for all that you have done for me.' He sat at the dining table and Sébastien joined him.

'There is nothing to pay back, though I do have a small request.'

'Of course, anything.' Nik nodded.

'My children would really like a kangaroo or koala soft toy.'

Nik grinned from ear to ear. 'Write down your address and I will arrange delivery of the toys for your children.' Nik drained the rest of his beer. 'What about you and your wife? Would you like something from Australia?'

'*Non*, just the children. They love anything to do with Australia, especially the animals.'

Nik chuckled. 'They are popular with the kids at home too.'

Sébastien checked his watch, finished his beer and rose to his feet. 'I must leave, or my wife will berate me for being late for dinner. Call me if you need anything, and contact Odette if you leave the house so she can redirect the surveillance cameras. Though I would recommend you do not go out. Ever since the terrorist attack in 2015, security videos are installed on every street and monitored twenty-four hours a day.'

'I will keep that in mind. Thanks, Sébastien.'

'Ring me when you need more food and supplies.'

'If there is a store close by, I can go and buy food.'

'*Non*, there are none close, and remember that the police are still looking for you.'

'Do you know if the park has cameras?'

'Why?'

'I thought it would be a good place to exercise.'

'Odette will find out for you,' Sébastien replied.

'Of course.' Nik nodded.

'Okay, *bonne chance* in finding your grandfather, my friend.'

Nik shook his hand. 'Thank you, my friend.'

Sébastien left, leaving Nik alone. He glanced around his new lodgings and wandered from room to room and upstairs to the main bedroom. He returned to the kitchen and made a toasted sandwich. Tomorrow, he would recommence his search.

CHAPTER 16

'Odette, I'm about two streets away from the antique store,' said Nik as he slowed his pace and scanned the various buildings and pedestrians' faces. He waited, hearing her click away on the keyboard.

'All clear,' she said.

Nik resumed walking, surveying the area for police and the Interpol agents. A rapid patter of footfalls on the pavement behind him drew closer. The hair on the back of his neck tingled and he resisted the urge to hasten his gait. A whiff of floral perfume wafted on the gentle breeze. Nik drew in a quick breath. A well-dressed woman in a slim-line skirt and sleeveless blouse strode past him. He watched her as she forged ahead and sighed in relief as she went around the corner.

'Did something happen?' asked Odette with concern.

'No.'

'I like your unshaven appearance,' Odette commented over the phone. 'Now you will fit in with the other young men.'

He came to an intersection, the pedestrian lights red. Nik did a casual sweep behind him and when the lights changed to green, he crossed the street. 'I thought about going blond.'

'*Oui*, with your blue eyes, you would be more handsome, but you will draw too much attention. Best not dye it. Perhaps you should let it grow longer,' Odette suggested.

'I had considered growing my hair.' Nik drew to a halt. 'I've arrived. I'll talk to you later.'

He slid the mobile phone into the pocket of his jacket and entered the shop. Over the past week he had visited the other antique stores his grandfather had called at, to establish a timeline and trigger point for his abduction. Odette used her skills to hack into the surveillance systems, enabling him to be invisible. He wanted to return to the antique store in Marseilles and speak to the shop owner, the last known sighting of his grandfather. Odette had protested, citing the police would be expecting him to return to the port city. He thought Detective Sauveterre would have posted undercover police at the other antique stores and was surprised that she hadn't.

He paused, his ears twitching, and flexed his fingers. It was as if someone was boring a hole between his shoulder blades. He could almost hear Odette say, 'I told you so'. There was no time to ponder who was watching him. He pushed the door open and the bell jingled. The old man looked up.

'*Bonjour*, monsieur.'

'*Bonjour*.' Nik walked to the counter as he took a photo of his grandfather from his wallet. 'I was here a few weeks ago asking if this man had come into your store.'

The old man frowned and shook his head.

'This is my grandfather. I am trying to find him.'

The man's eyes widened. 'You are the man the police are searching for.' The owner reached for the phone. Quick as lightning, Nik wrenched the receiver away and tossed it aside. He grasped the old man's wrist. The old man winced.

'You were not honest with me last time.' Nik held up the photo. 'Did this man come into your store?'

The owner shrank back and tried to pull his hand from Nik's vice-like grip. 'I cannot help you.' He glanced over Nik's shoulder towards the door, breathing fast.

Nik released his hand and the older man stumbled and almost toppled over. Moving quickly, Nik wove around pieces of furniture as he headed for the rear of the shop. He concealed himself behind two tall bookcases, adrenaline coursing through his veins. The bell on the door chimed.

'*Halte!* Police!' a voice commanded.

Nik plucked the coin from the front pocket of his jeans and flipped it in the air. Wind spiralled around him and buffeted his body as he was barrelled into the familiar maelstrom that propelled him through the infinitesimal dimension between space and time.

He landed on his back, gasping. He blinked, his vision filled with white blinding lights, similar to a camera flash. The bright blue cloudless sky came into view as his sight cleared. Something sharp was poking him in the back. With a grunt, he reached for the offending object, tossed the rock aside and slumped back, eyes closed, the sun warming his face.

He lay there on the grass, breathing the fresh air. He turned his head from one side to the other and grinned, recognising the hedging running along the backyard of the house where he was staying. He was in the park. Nik sat up, his head clear and body relaxed. Better than hitting a piece of furniture, he thought, rubbing his back as he stood. With more practice, he would learn to land on his feet.

Nik trudged along the hedge until he reached the street, and walked past the two neighbouring houses to get to his lodgings. Once inside, he shrugged off his jacket and climbed the stairs, stripping and dropping his clothes on the floor on the way to the bathroom. He stood under the hot water streaming from the shower head, the stinging spray easing the physical aches. He found showering after a teleport helped to relax his muscles. After drying off, he collapsed onto the bed and fell asleep.

———

He was woken by sound of his mobile phone ringing and another noise. Nik sat up dazed and groggy, the sound of banging clearer.

'Nik!' someone shouted, the voice muffled through the door.

He got up and pulled on a t-shirt and jeans. At the bottom of the stairs, the front door vibrated from the insistent hammering. He looked through the peephole before opening the door.

'Odette? What are you—'

The petite woman burst through the entry her face contorted in panic. 'Don't you answer your phone? I was worried the police had captured you! You need to answer your phone! I didn't know if something happened to you.' She glowered at him.

'I apologise for scaring you, but you didn't need to come all this way,' he said.

Odette crossed her arms against her chest. 'You disappeared. I couldn't track you, and when you didn't return my call, I thought something had happened.' Her lips pursed.

'As you can see, I'm fine and I didn't get arrested.'

She thumped him on the chest. 'How did you get back here without my help?'

'Ouch.' Nik looked at her in surprise and took a step back. He headed down the passage and went into the kitchen. 'I had to get away quick and stole a motorbike.'

'How did you escape from the shop? From what I saw on the security camera footage, there was no way out.' Her eyes narrowed.

'There was an emergency exit hidden behind a row of

bookshelves.' He took out coffee cups from the overhead cupboard and set them on the kitchen bench. 'Not very smart or safe if the place caught on fire, and I had to wedge myself through the small opening to avoid getting caught.' He filled the filter and made them both a coffee.

'Detective Sauveterre was there.' Odette eyed him with interest. He handed her a cup of brewed coffee.

Nik leaned against the counter and took a sip of his coffee. 'That's no surprise. She would have predicted I'd return to the store. She had her team follow me there the first time.'

'She is determined to catch you.' Odette wandered into the living room and sat on the sofa.

'I expected no less from her. She's doing her job.' He sat in the adjacent armchair. 'How did you get here? I thought you didn't drive.'

'You thought wrong,' she said. 'I drove here on my Vespa.'

'You shouldn't have risked coming here. I would have called you back.'

'I wouldn't be here if you had picked up the phone,' she said, wagging her finger at him. 'I tried for two hours before deciding to check on you.'

Nik picked up his discarded jacket and pulled out the mobile. She had rung his number every five minutes in the timeframe she mentioned. 'I'm sorry, Odette, I didn't hear the phone. I left my jacket down here when I went upstairs and I fell asleep.'

'You're not telling me everything. Where is the motorbike?' she asked.

'I left it in a shopping centre car park and walked the rest of the way.'

She tapped her foot. 'How did you avoid the cameras?'

'I kept my back to the cameras, and where possible walked in the shade or between buildings.'

'What if someone recognised you?' she asked, glowering at him.

'I wasn't recognised.'

'How can you be certain?' she asked, exasperated.

'If you didn't see me on the streets, then the police certainly didn't,' he answered.

She stared into her coffee cup. '*Oui*, you are correct, I would have seen you.' She placed the cup on the coffee table. 'What is tomorrow's destination?'

'Given the close call today, I think we hold off for a day before I head for Geneva. That is where my grandfather and I had identified where Resnik began his search for rare coins. Are you able to break into the security systems in other countries?'

Odette raised a brow at him and frowned. 'How are you going to get into Geneva? It's unwise to use the trains, buses or taxis, even in your disguise. The brown-coloured contacts and the beard may have fooled them this time, but they will eventually identify you with the facial recognition software.'

'I'll work something out,' he said.

'Maybe Sébastien can take you,' she suggested.

'No, I'll find a way,' Nik said with a firm shake of his head.

'It will be impossible for you to enter Geneva, unless you are planning to steal another motorcycle,' she said.

'Or buy one,' he said, his eyes lighting up. 'That would work.'

'*Non*. The police will identify you as soon as you enter a motorcycle shop.' Odette stood. 'I will arrange a motorbike for you and have Sébastien bring it here.'

'Odette, I can't have you buying a motorbike for me,' he protested.

She shrugged. 'It will be a gift from my government as recompense for your grandfather being kidnapped.' She started for the front door, with Nik following. 'Ring me if you need anything else for your trip, and never make me check on you again.'

'I'll do that. And Odette.' She turned to him. 'Thank you.'

CHAPTER 17

Nik and Sébastien were sitting at the kitchen table with a map of Geneva. It had taken Odette a few days to arrange for the purchase of a motorcycle using the fake ID she had created for Nik. A brand-new white Triumph sat in the driveway.

'I should come with you,' said Sébastien as the two men reviewed the route. 'There are tolls and you need a passport to cross into Switzerland.'

'Not with this EU Blue Card Odette created for me.'

The Frenchman leaned across the table and picked up the card. 'You don't have brown eyes.'

'Not yet.' Nik tapped on a small box. 'But I will with these coloured contact lens.'

'A man travelling alone is more, how do you say, suspect than two people,' argued Sébastien.

Nik grasped his friend's shoulder and gave a reassuring squeeze. 'I understand your concern, Sébastien, and I am truly grateful, but this is my grandfather and my responsibility.' He peered at Sébastien and waited for him to nod. 'Besides, you will want to be home when those fluffy toys arrive,' Nik added with a smile and poked him in the chest. 'I want to see the photos when your children open the parcels. You don't want to miss opportunities like those, they are priceless, which you must enjoy before they get old enough to go to high school. After that, they won't want anything to do with you.'

Sébastien shook his head. 'You teach high school students, *oui?*'

Nik nodded. 'Two weeks into the school term.' He stared at the map, his face darkening. 'Resnik's abduction of my grandfather was a terrible decision.'

Sébastien gazed at him, worried. 'Promise me you won't do anything you will regret.'

The rim of the ancient coin in his jeans pocket dug into Nik's hip. He was getting used to its presence and the constant reminder of his role as guardian. The downside of not using the coin was not being familiar with or knowing the layout of the destination. Was there a way to teleport from one place to an unfamiliar site? Perhaps, perhaps not.

'I do not care about being caught. I want to get my grandfather back.' Nik folded the map. 'Any other tips for the trip to Geneva?'

Sébastien eyed him. 'We drive quite fast but don't go more than ten kilometres over the speed limit. And while Odette can manipulate the cameras, the highway patrol is a constant presence on the A6.'

'Good to know. Thank you.'

'Let me come with you,' Sébastien pleaded. 'You are not familiar with our roads or laws.'

'I'll be fine, Sébastien. Besides, Odette will be watching and no doubt alert you if something goes wrong.'

Sébastien pressed his lips together and muttered in French. He picked up his keys. 'Call me if you need anything.' He stood and nodded at Nik.

'I will.'

'*Adieu*, Nik.'

'*Adieu*, Sébastien.'

The next day, Nik left Paris at 6 am in the morning and it took him five and a half hours to arrive in Geneva. The trip was uneventful. As he drove along Rue de Chantepoulet, he came to an intersection and turned right onto Rue de Mont-Blanc, which became Pont du Mont-Blanc, the main road that led into the centre of the city. He noted the architecture around the waterfront was reminiscent of the apartment buildings in Paris. He followed the Rhone River until it merged into Lake Geneva, the largest lake in the Alps. Boats and cruisers bobbed on the glassy surface like beached seals, the turquoise waters shimmering in the early afternoon sunlight.

'Odette, I'm about to drive over Pont du Mont-Blanc and onto Rue Francois-Versonnex where the coin store is located,' Nik said into his headset.

'Okay.'

He heard a few taps on the keyboard.

'Go ahead, the way is clear,' she said. After a few seconds she asked, 'Did you see any police?'

Nik changed gears, the engine revs slowing as he approached the intersection. 'There were a number of patrols on the highway, and I kept to the speed limit as Sébastien suggested.' He glanced across the lake. 'This is a beautiful city. It's a pity I'm not here to sightsee.'

'Geneva is a wonderful place to visit, and they speak French.'

'As well as Italian, German and Romantsch dialects and English. It helps to be on good terms with your neighbours.' He released the brake and took off as the lights turned green.

'You should see the store soon,' she said.

'Yes, I can see the sign on the shop-front. It's not a big place.' He pulled over, parked across from the store and raised the visor on his helmet. 'I'm going in.'

'Leave your phone on,' Odette said.

'Odette, there is no need,' he said tapping the button on the Bluetooth headset and pulling off the helmet.

'You are too far for either me or Sébastien to aid you if something happens. This way, I can listen to everything and if anything occurs, I can call Sébastien.'

He sighed and crossed the busy road. 'Fine.'

Nik entered the store and approached the counter.

'*Monsieur, comment puis-je vous aider aujourd'hui?*' the shopkeeper asked.

'*Monsieur, pardon, je ne parle ... pas bien ... le français. Parlez-vous anglais?*' Nik replied in halting French, trying to remember the phrase Odette had taught him.

'Of course, monsieur. How may I help you today?'

'I was wondering if you had any Ancient Greek coins in your collection?'

'We have a few.'

'May I have a look please?' he asked.

'I have accessed the store's camera and can see you,' Odette told him.

'Certainly. One moment.' The storekeeper stepped away from the counter and disappeared into another room. While he waited, Nik looked around the store and noting the location of the camera. The collection of coins and jewellery labelled with origins and price were locked inside glass cabinets, each secured with independent alarms.

'Here we are,' the man said, returning. He placed the encased coins, spaced two fingers apart and ensconced in their felt bed, onto the counter.

Nik examined them, and saw they were from a later period

than the one he carried. 'I'm sorry, they are not from the era I'm interested in. Thank you for your time.' He paused. 'Do you recall if an older man in his seventies came into your store some weeks ago?'

'There was an English gentleman, a professor he claimed, who came enquiring after Greek coins. I suggested he go to the antique store on Rue des Barques.'

'Thank you.' Nik nodded at the man and left the store. 'Odette, did you hear that?'

'*Oui.*' There was a pause. 'I suggest you don't waste time,' she warned. 'He is about to call the police.'

'What makes you think he is ringing the police?' he asked, getting back on the motorbike.

'As I was watching through the store camera, I saw the expression on his face. He recognised you and picked up the phone as soon as you left.'

'Even with my disguise? Dammit! Can you block the call or make it ring out?' he asked, checking the traffic before merging and moving across the lanes to do a left-hand turn on the next street.

'I'm navigating the phone system right now,' she replied. 'You'll need to work on your disguise. Perhaps a much fuller beard and longer hair may help.'

'Maybe,' Nik grunted, not entirely convinced. 'Am I cleared for the streets to Rue des Barques?'

'*Juste moi une* minute,' came the strained response.

'I don't have a minute, Odette. If I go any slower, I'll draw the attention of the local constabulary, and that's not a good idea.' He trailed behind a delivery van, staying in sight of the driver's side mirror. 'Odette? We're cutting this a little close.' His gut churned and beads of sweat formed on his chest and stuck to his T-shirt under his leather jacket. 'Odette? Now would be a good time!'

'Done!' she cried out.

Nik checked the mirror for nearby vehicles before indicating and changing lanes. A tall well-built man with a blond crewcut was walking along the sidewalk on the same side as the coin store when he turned onto the street. Nik parked the motorbike and sat with the engine idling.

'This is the place,' he said.

'Are you sure?' asked Odette.

'Yes. I saw Resnik's new bodyguard walk into the shop. I'm going to follow him when he leaves.'

'He's a dangerous man, Nik,' she warned.

'You have done some research on him?'

'*Oui*. This man is an assassin and on Interpol's watch-list,' she replied. He heard her mutter and swear.

'Do you have a name?' Nik frowned when she didn't reply. 'Odette, what is his name?'

'Wilhelm Ritterbusch. He is the descendant of Fritz Ritterbusch, one of the Obersturmfuhrers at Flossenbürg, a concentration camp in Bavaria.'

A quiver of unease skittered up his spine, like the delicate legs of a spider. He knew about many of the concentration camps from his studies at university. From the historical accounts, prisoners sent to Flossenbürg were men with alleged asocial tendencies, others were supposed criminal offenders, as well as incarcerated outspoken Germans with anti-Hitler political views.

'Now I know who I'm dealing with,' he said matter-of-fact.

'As much as I despise the police, I think you should let them find your grandfather,' she suggested.

'It will be okay, Odette. I know what I'm doing.'

'These are ruthless men, Nik, and you are not familiar with the region,' she argued.

'That's why I have you,' he said. 'You are my digital eyes and ears, and you can keep me from being tailed.'

'After all the research and Intel we have collected on Resnik, we know he doesn't abduct people without cause. Your grandfather must be important—'

'Ritterbusch is leaving the store and heading back along Rue de la Scie, towards Lake Geneva. Can you track him?' Nik interrupted. He waited until the German halted for the traffic on Quai Gustave-Ador and then crossed the road to follow him.

'He's making his way towards the park,' she replied.

'Son of a—!' Nik cursed as he hit the brakes, the lights against him at the intersection.

When they turned green, he changed gears to overtake a vehicle. He sped across the four-lane road, and slowed at the pedestrian crossing that led into the park. He drove into a car park, cut the engine, pulled off his helmet and hurried to catch up with Resnik's bodyguard.

The verdant park bustled with people picnicking and enjoying the afternoon sunshine. Donning his sunglasses, Nik walked past a bust of Gustave Ador, President of the Confederation in 1919, and glimpsed the tall blond man nearing a gazebo. He lengthened his stride and came within ten metres of the German when he stooped to have a drink at the fountain. Nik deviated to the right and kept to the path as it skirted the fountain and wound its way back towards the lake. He joined other pedestrians on the promenade and stole a glance at the large fountain of the four seasons, the water sprouting from two tiers of sculptures, four cherubs on the top half and at the base four statues representing the Greek gods and goddesses.

'No! No! No!' Nik scanned the area.

'What happened?' asked Odette.

'I've lost him.' Nik cut across the manicured grass and followed the line of trees to another gazebo that led to an outdoor restaurant. 'Spotted him.'

Nik watched the German breeze past diners and enter the bistro. He wavered, reached into his jeans pocket, the coin vibrating in his palm. He clenched his hand around the coin, the tingling and drumming threading along the nerves in his arm. The sensation spreading across his shoulders and torso was akin to pins and needles. Nik unclenched his hand and glanced at his palm, astonished. The imprint had bitten deeply into his palm. An angry red mark marred his skin, as if he had been scalded.

'Nik? What's going on?'

'Huh?'

'What's happening? Did you catch up with Ritterbusch?'

'No, he got away from me. He went into a restaurant and that's where I lost him.' Nik slid the coin into his pocket and rubbed his hand up and down his leg.

'Oh, I'm sorry, Nik.' Odette began typing. 'Shall I start on securing the route from your current location?'

Nik swore, annoyed at losing sight of Ritterbusch. 'Okay, Odette.' He turned about face and headed back to the motorbike.

'Are you alright, Nik?'

'Yes, I'm fine.'

CHAPTER 18

Darkness loomed not too far behind the hint of purple hues on the horizon as Nik returned to the house after the long drive from Geneva. He trudged through the door and went straight upstairs. Nik wished he could talk to his grandfather about his experiences with the coin. Papou would have some explanation for why it had behaved the way it did.

After he showered, he stretched out on the bed, a forearm resting across his forehead. Nik held the ancient artefact up to the light and studied both sides, trying to figure out why it had pulsated. The coin hadn't vibrated or made his palm burn when he used it, except for the initial harsh side-effects from the first few teleportations. He loathed going against his grandfather's wishes and using the relic, but considering the current situation, he reckoned he had a good reason to harness its power.

He rolled the coin over his knuckles. *Was it something to do with the unusual metal properties of the coin?*

The alloys were a mystery. During the Middle Ages Theon the alchemist conducted many experiments on the coin and was unable to identify or recognise the elements. It was possible the previous guardians also did not understand the magnitude of the coins' powers. One coin on its own was formidable, the power of the two together would be perilous and have catastrophic consequences. He slid the coin under his pillow and rolled onto his side. For now, he needed to sleep. Tomorrow, with a clear mind, he would ponder the conundrum of his unique charge.

Nik was leaning against the kitchen island drinking a cup of espresso and staring at the coin when the front door opened.

'*Bonjour*, Monsieur Nik!'

Nik slipped the coin into his pocket of his chinos. '*Bonjour*, Sébastien. I'm in the kitchen,' he replied and turned to greet his friend.

Sébastien dropped his car keys on the table and set down a tray of mixed breakfast pastries on the kitchen bench. He picked out two pastries and put them in the microwave.

'Best served warm,' he said.

When the microwave pinged, he put one on a plate and offered it to Nik. Nik took a bite and the thick velvety chocolate burst into his mouth coating his tongue and teeth.

'That is superb,' he said, swallowing and licking his teeth.

'*Oui*, the best *pain au chocolat*,' beamed Sébastien. Nik passed him a cup of coffee and they sat at the dining table. 'Odette tells me you saw Resnik's new man.'

'Yes, and the bastard got away. I wish I'd caught up with him.'

'Given Odette's research, she says he is a dangerous man.'

'Resnik's former bodyguard was also an assassin and he was killed,' stated Nik.

'*Oui*, but Detective Sauveterre shot him,' Sébastien pointed out.

'True, except if she hadn't interfered, my grandfather and I would be back home.'

Sébastien bit his bottom lip. 'Perhaps you should let the detective find your grandfather.'

'Now you sound like Odette.'

'I have less affection for the police than she does,' said Sébastien, 'but you may get hurt or executed. Then your family loses two people, and that would be a tragedy for them and for me. I regard you as a friend, and Odette would also be unhappy if anything happened to you.'

'I cannot do that, my grandfather is my responsibility,' Nik said. 'I appreciate your concern. You were there when I tried to talk to Detective Sauveterre. She wanted to arrest me.'

Sébastien sat back in his chair. 'What are your plans?'

'I'm going to Rome. I will ask Odette to book a room at a hotel for me today.'

Sébastien gaped at him. 'Why Rome?'

'There were a couple of antique stores on my grandfather's list,' Nik replied.

'Do you think Resnik will send Ritterbusch to Rome?'

Nik shrugged. 'It's likely he would. There are a few stores on Via dei Coronari I want to visit before Resnik orders Ritterbusch to Rome.'

'I don't know, Monsieur Nik, you are, how do you say ... flying blind. You are guessing Resnik will send his man to Rome. What if he doesn't, then what? Contact Detective Sauveterre, she is your best hope to locate your grandfather, and she has the backing of the police to deal with a man like Resnik,' Sébastien advised.

'What if she arrests me? Then I can't help my grandfather.' Nik's hand tightened around the small coffee cup.

'Offer her information she may not have,' Sébastien suggested. 'Intel she cannot uncover through the police network.'

Nik's knee bounced up and down. 'I'll think about it.'

'You must stay alive for your family.'

After Sébasatien left, Nik sat outside in the backyard, mulling over what he'd said. There was a way to find out where Ritterbusch was travelling, but it required using the coin. He was reluctant to do that, not after what happened in Geneva. He scrutinised the coin. It lay inert on his palm, a flat grey mass.

No tingling or vibration.

CHAPTER 19

Nik paced back and forward from the kitchen to the entrance of the house, his jaw clenched. He pondered what to do and which of the two options to choose. Both had potentially different outcomes, one more desirable than the other. He stomped back towards the front of the house and stared out onto the quiet street, his mobile phone in one hand and the coin in the other. With one quick flip he could retrieve the necessary information, but if he used the coin would it alert Ritterbusch? And could the German track the coin's trajectory to him and his location, just as he and his grandfather were able to pinpoint the sister coin's trail? The alternative was not better either. If he called the detective, she would apprehend him, just as she had attempted to do at Disneyland.

He returned to the kitchen, flung the phone onto the dining table where it skidded along the surface, hitting and bouncing off the ceramic vase. Nik pulled off his T-shirt, tossed it onto a chair, and went outside and started doing push-ups. The advantage he had over Resnik was that the terrorist could not find him. Not yet anyway.

The muscles in his shoulders and biceps contracted with each move, levering his body up and down with ease. After thirty minutes he stopped, his chest and face sheathed in sweat, droplets splashing on the grass beneath him. He stood, wiped his brow with the back of his hand and marched into the house.

Nik's hand closed around the coin and his body swayed from side to side, as if he were sitting in a dinghy on a river. He looked around in amazement and smiled: the jump had been successful.

He waited a few seconds for his equilibrium to settle before sitting down at the bank of computers in his grandfather's secret basement. Everything seemed different to him, the library of rare and precious books, the extensive range of weapons dating back to the 1500 BCE, including King Leonidas of Sparta's armour, sword, shield and greaves, right to the twenty-first century Kevlar vest and armoury. The hermetic room was filled with rare papyri from Ancient Egypt, Ancient Greece, Mesopotamia, Ancient Rome, through to the mediaeval period. The dichotomy of the armoury—past and present—struck Nik as ironic. No matter how advanced technology developed, some things remain the same. Mankind always looked for better ways to defend and kill each other.

Now he understood what his grandfather had endeavoured to make him grasp, and what it meant to be a guardian of Aphrodite's coin. The role was more than just being a protector. The guardian was also caretaker of the world's history. If Resnik stole the sister coin, the implications for humanity could be worse than Hitler's attempt at world domination.

Nik typed in the new locations Odette had identified when she hacked into various databases. The computers started pinging straightaway. Nik took screenshots of the feeds and locations of where the sister coin and its user had traversed. Apart from Geneva there were three other sites the jumper returned to often. He sent the files to the printer.

While he waited, Nik walked to the weapons cabinet, typed in the code on the panel and stepped back as the glass door hissed ajar. He pulled out a TASER and grabbed a box of ammunition, and slid both into his backpack. He secured the door, collected the printouts and moved to the centre of the room. Nik tossed the coin into the air.

A fresh, light breeze washed over his face and arms, the scent of grass and perfumed roses greeted him. Nik opened his eyes and almost whooped out loud but instead did a victory punch in the air. He had returned to the backyard of the house he was staying with no mishaps, just a mild wooziness from the teleportation. He checked his watch and saw that he had been gone for over two hours.

'Crap.' He hurried inside and dialled a number on his phone. '*Bonjour*, Odette. Were you able to get me a pass for the Francois-Mitterrand library?'

'*Oui*. You have access to Room J. It's located on the philosophy, history and human sciences floor.'

'Perfect. Are you able to guide me to the library?'

'*Oui*, and you had better leave now. The traffic across the city at this time of the afternoon is slow and bumper to bumper.'

'Right. It's fortunate I have the motorbike. Give me fifteen minutes.'

He dashed up the stairs to his bedroom, taking them two steps at a time and hid the extra ammunition and TASER in his suitcase, with the revolver and knife, passport and laptop. He removed a document wallet and thrust it into his backpack. Nik replaced the extra pillows and blankets on top of the suitcase. Next, he went into the bathroom and put in the coloured contact lenses. He snatched up the backpack from the floor and left the house. He pulled on the helmet, tapped on the headset and reconnected with Odette.

'Let's do this.'

'Wow, this is an amazing library,' said Nik, awed as he stared up at the four looming towers that resembled open books. He adjusted the cords of his ear buds and moved the mic closer to his mouth.

'It's the biggest in the world,' Odette commented with a hint of pride in her voice.

'Which way to the public library?' he asked.

'You are near the western entrance. Go inside and up the ramps to the Upper Garden Level and you will see the library. At the reception desk, check in your pass and I'll guide you from there,' she said.

'Right.' Nik entered the library and gaped. The slick design and lighting reminded him of a shopping mall. The south-facing windows overlooked an interior park encircled by the four towers. Corridors with wooden floors and spacious carpeted areas separated the various zones. He almost walked past the reception desk, astounded by the enormous structure and the busyness of the place, and had to backtrack a few steps. He waited until beckoned, showed his card and was admitted into the library.

'Which way to Room J, Odette?' he asked in a soft tone.

'Walk straight ahead until you reach the end of the corridor,' she said. 'I've booked the group room for you.'

'Do you think it's a good idea to leave the information in the room? Won't someone go in if they see the space is free?' he whispered.

'I have arranged it with the librarian in charge, no-one will enter the room. Ask for Elayne at the enquiries desk, she's expecting you.'

'What an extraordinary library,' he murmured. 'The collection must be in the millions.'

'It has over forty million resources, many of the historical documents and rare manuscripts date back to the Middle Ages, which are archived on the upper floors.'

'Incredible. This would be a great place to do research.'

Odette laughed.

'What's so funny?' he asked.

'You sounded just like a teacher.'

Nik approached the enquiries desk and took out one of his ear buds but remained on the phone with Odette. '*Bonjour*, please excuse me for my lack of French-speaking skills. I was wondering if I could speak to Elayne?'

The svelte pretty and youthful brunette gave him an appraising once-over.

'Odette didn't mention how handsome you are,' she said, her green-blue eyes twinkling. She thrust out a hand. 'I am Elayne.'

Nik smiled and shook her hand. 'Thank you for booking the room for me.'

'Of course. When Odette contacted me with her unusual request, I was curious.'

'She's a good friend.' He looked around the library space. 'You must be exceptional at your job to be appointed to a senior position for someone who's as young as you,' he remarked.

'Not only attractive but a charmer too. Would you like to get a coffee at the café after I have done this good deed for you?'

Nik heard Odette mutter in disbelief. He passed Elayne the sealed envelope with the detective's name on the front.

'Perhaps another time,' he answered.

She scrawled her name and phone number on the back of a business card and held it out to him. 'Call me for that, next time.'

Nik smiled a little self-consciously, aware that Odette could hear every exchange. '*Merci beaucoup*, Elayne.' He turned to leave, and sucked in a quick breath when he saw a familiar figure at the far end of the corridor.

'What is it?' Odette and Elayne asked at the same time.

'The detective.' He spun around to the librarian. 'Is there another way out of here?'

'*Oui*. Head over to the history section.' She pointed to the furthest section of the library. 'I will come for you after I have spoken to the detective.'

Nik strolled across to the other side of the library, his heart beating a rapid drumroll, and took a deep breath before stepping behind a line of bookshelves. He rubbed the back of his neck and checked his watch. Nik cursed under his breath, annoyed at the detective for arriving early, and at himself for not learning from his trip to Disneyland and how she had set him up.

'What's taking her so long?' he muttered, his gaze darting between the gaps of the books. He resisted the urge to peek around the shelving to see what was happening. 'Can we trust her?'

'*Oui*, though I did not expect Elayne to ask you out for a coffee,' came back the sharp response.

'Good to know we can trust her,' he whispered, taking a book from a shelf as a person entered the aisle. He started flicking through its pages, pausing every few pages to peer through the shelving. His ears pricked at the sound of fingers clacking against keyboards on laptops, the squeaky wheels on a book cart, and the low tones of people talking. He flipped to the cover of the book and saw it was about the French Revolution. At another time he would like to read it, but the proximity of the detective quashed his enthusiasm.

'*Je suis désolé* ... I'm sorry.' Nik swung around at Elayne's harried voice. She hastened towards him, hands wringing. 'The detective kept asking a lot of questions, she was very insistent. I did my best to answer her. Come this way.' She took him by the hand and led him along the rear of the room and around to the elevator. 'Kiss me.'

'What?'

The elevator doors opened.

'The detective is looking in the opposite direction, and soon she will turn. Get into the elevator and kiss me,' she urged, pulling him into the lift.

Nik peered over her shoulder and recognised the detective. He wrapped his arms around Elayne and wheeled them about, his back towards the library. Elayne clasped her arms around his neck and kissed him. The doors closed, the lift juddered and glided upwards.

'That was a little too close,' Nik said letting her go.

'She knew it was you who gave me the envelope and asked if you were still in the library.'

'What did you tell her?'

'I told her a man dropped off the package and left without saying another word.'

'What else did she ask?'

'For a description.'

Nik tensed.

She beamed at him. 'Don't worry, I didn't give you away. But I said I had to leave as my boyfriend was waiting for me and gets impatient if I'm late.'

'I don't know,' he frowned, rubbing his unshaven jaw. 'Detective Sauveterre doesn't strike me as someone who would accept your story of meeting a boyfriend. It's too convenient of an excuse.'

'You mean to say as a librarian, I wouldn't have a boyfriend who I'm meeting for a coffee?' Elayne scowled at him, her hands on her hips.

'That's not what I meant at all. I would be more surprised if you didn't have a boyfriend. The reason you gave is too neat though, especially as it's on the same day I arranged for the detective to pick up the documents.' He glanced at the numbers flashing as they passed the floors. 'She will be able to follow us.'

Elayne shook her head. 'Only library staff are permitted to enter the other floors in the building.'

'She's a detective, she just needs to show her badge to gain access,' he said. 'Where are we going?'

'We will get out at the next level, walk along the mezzanine to Tower of Time, then into the garden,' she replied.

CHAPTER 20

The doors slid open. Elayne took his hand again and grinned up at him.

'We must keep up the pretence of you being my boyfriend in case my colleagues stop us and ask who you are.'

Odette sighed out loud in Nik's ear bud. 'Next, she will say you are her fiancé.'

Nik snorted back a laugh, covered his mouth and coughed. Given the precariousness and absurdity of his predicament, it was difficult not to react to Odette's comment.

'How much further?' he asked, as they sped along the open space. He looked back from where they had come and to the other three buildings. 'We are too exposed. We can't hide with all these windows, and the detective can see where we're going.'

'That's why I'm taking you to the park. There are lots of places to hide.'

'I don't want to hide, I want to leave,' he said.

They came to a staircase and began their descent.

'Elayne?' a man said.

Nik cringed as they stopped to greet the newcomer.

'*Bonjour*, Jacques.' She continued speaking to the man in French, with Odette translating that she was showing her new English boyfriend around the library.

Nik smiled at Jacques, who looked to be in his mid-forties, and did not appear too pleased by Elayne's explanation. He stuck out his hand.

'*Bonjour, monsieur*, I apologise for breaking the rules. It's not Elayne's fault. I was excited to see the architecture of the building as it is unique and the largest library in the world,' he said in his best British accent. 'I'm a bit of a library buff, having seen the new Alexandria library. Now that is a marvel of engineering. When I learned Elayne,' he pulled her closer and kissed her on the cheek, 'worked in this magical location, I pleaded with her to show me around.' He beamed at her. 'I was very persuasive, wasn't I?'

Elayne leaned into him and smiled coyly. '*Oui*, you were rather insistent, and difficult to refuse.'

Jacques' brows furrowed. 'You had better move along. If Monsieur Barreau finds you here, he will fire you, Elayne.'

'Best we move along then, honey,' Nik said. 'I don't want you to get into trouble with the boss, not on my account.' He nodded at the other man. They dashed down the stairs, Elayne giving directions. At a set of glass sliding doors she scanned her security card and they opened out into the gardens.

She led the way to a cluster of trees. Her cheeks were flushed and her eyes sparkled. 'That was exhilarating!'

'I think we were lucky it was Jacques and not your boss who saw us,' Nik said. 'By the way, Jacques likes you.'

Elayne guffawed. 'Jacques? He's not my type. Besides, he's older than me.'

'He's keen on you, otherwise he wouldn't have let us leave,' said Nik.

'Jacques? Really? He's rather bookish.'

Nik laughed. 'Says one librarian about another librarian.'

'I'm not your stereotypical librarian,' she said, pouting.

'No, you're not.' Nik gave her a hug. 'Besides, librarians do amazing work.'

'We do.'

'This is an impressive green space,' he said, appraising the verdant enclosure. Birds twittered overhead, the sound interspersed with the rustling of the treetops. It was a serene and comforting space despite the busy location being encircled by main roads. 'Where to from here?'

'Did you come on the train or bus?'

'I drove here and parked my motorbike on Rue Raymond Aron.'

She gawked at him. 'Do you have a girlfriend? If you don't, I'm happy to fulfil that role!'

He gave her a lopsided grin. 'That's flattering, but my life is rather complex at present and I have no time for a relationship.'

Elayne's face crumpled.

'When I resolve my business, how about you, me and Odette go out for dinner, as a thank you for your help and for almost losing your job.'

'That would be lovely,' she said, brightening. She pointed. 'This is the way out and it will take you back to the west entrance.'

It took them ten minutes of walking at a brisk pace to reach the other end of the park. Elayne scanned her card through the slot next to the glass doors. They descended an iron staircase that zigzagged down the building and came out beneath the mezzanine floor. Bright sunlight flooded the space and warmed the otherwise austere metal structure. She led him to revolving doors that opened into the main lobby.

'Through those doors is Rue Raymond Aron,' she said.

'Thank you again, Elayne. I owe you a great debt of gratitude,' he said, kissing her on the cheek.

She beamed. 'I look forward to our dinner.'

Nik set off towards the doors, merging with other library patrons.

'Mademoiselle Elayne!' called out a familiar voice.

'You had better move,' said Odette, the sound of her clacking away at the keyboard coming through loud and clear.

'How the hell did she find Elayne?' His pulse raced and he took longer strides. 'We remained out of sight.'

'Except when Jacques saw you,' answered Odette.

'Do you think he said something to the detective?'

'I would say that he did,' she said in a mild tone.

'I knew eluding the detective was too easy.'

Nik stole a glance over his shoulder and saw the young librarian engaged in an animated conversation with Detective Sauveterre. From the officer's posture, it seemed clear that Elayne's explanation did not convince her. He watched the detective examine the crowd and then start circling around towards his location. Nik scampered through the door and scooted down the stairs, taking them two at a time. He raced across the wide footpath and darted across Rue Raymond Aron to Rue Fernand Braudel, where he had parked his motorbike.

Nik pulled on his helmet and turned the key in the ignition. He peeked back at the library before taking off. The detective was at the top of the stairs scanning the street. Gunning the engine, he sped towards the end of the road, heeding Odette's directions.

CHAPTER 21

When he arrived back at the house, Nik sat on the motorbike, its engine idling, cursing himself for the close call. When was he going to learn the detective couldn't be trusted?

He turned off the engine. The couple next door were in their garden, the wife watering the flowers while the husband trimmed the roses. They smiled and waved at him. Nik waved back and removed his helmet.

'Beautiful day to be in the garden,' he said, alighting from the motorbike.

'*Oui.* You are enjoying the sights of Paris?' asked the husband.

Nik's mobile phone rang. He looked at the number displayed on the screen. 'My apologies,' he said. 'It's my father.'

'You better answer,' the neighbour said with a smile and returned to his pruning.

'Hi Dad, can I call you back in a sec?' Nik unlocked the front door and entered the house. He set the bike helmet down on the hallway table.

'Is there something wrong?' his dad asked.

'No, no. I'll call you.' He hung up and sank onto the settee, his head in his hands. He then dialled Odette's number. 'Odette, I need to call my parents. Can you make sure my new number isn't traced?'

'When was the last time you spoke to your father and mother?' she asked.

'The day I left the hotel,' he replied with a sigh.

'And you have not spoken to them since? Shame on you.'

'I've been busy,' he retorted. 'Also, I don't want my parents to get involved in what I'm doing. If they know what's happening it will be difficult for them to lie when the police contact them.'

'I understand your reasoning, but they would worry more not hearing from you,' she said, disapproval clear in her tone.

'Yes, I know.'

'Call your parents. I will work magic from here.'

'Thank you, Odette.'

Nik dialled his parents' number, his father answered on the third ring.

'Dad, don't hang up, it's me, Nik.'

'What's going on? I didn't recognise the number. That French police detective has been calling asking if we've heard from you and to ring her when we do. Your mother and I are worried. What is happening?'

Nik gave his father an overview of the situation, glossing over how the police suspected him and his grandfather of colluding with neo-Nazis. His father gave a few expletives when he finished.

'I've contacted a lawyer who specialises in international law and I'll let him know what's happening. He's going to contact the Australian Embassy and we hope to hear from him soon. What is it you need from us?' his father asked.

'If the detective calls again, refer her to the lawyer,' Nik said. 'Was there anything else she wanted to know?'

'She quizzed us about your friendships, your current workplace, and if you were in a relationship.'

'Huh ...' Nik rubbed his brow. 'Okay then. I'll ring you again soon.'

'Are you safe?' Nik heard his mother ask, her voice tinged with concern.

'I am, Mum. Love you both.'

'We love you too.'

Nik said goodbye and ended the call. He flopped back on the sofa, his head arched back, the muscles in his neck stretched taut, and thought about the questions the detective posed to his parents. She was gathering a profile on him. She wouldn't find much as there wasn't anything in his life to deduce evidence from, except for his new position as guardian of Aphrodite's coin, which no-one except he and his grandfather knew about.

The role of protecting an inanimate object was meant to be low key. That's what he thought, based on Papou's experience, until the alerts occurred, which had changed everything. Now it was a race to rescue his grandfather and to safeguard the coin. He yawned. Never had he felt this tired, not even from marking Ancient History essays into the early hours of the morning.

It was time to consider his next move. A lot depended on the detective's reaction to the research he left for her in the library. If he'd judged her character correctly, her sense of justice and morality could prove to be in his favour. If he hadn't, he would implement the next stage of his strategy.

Nik woke with a start. He flicked on the table lamp next to the couch and froze. Bright blue striations of light filtered through the glass panel on the front door, flooding the hallway. Muffled voices outside pervaded into the house. Nik grabbed his mobile phone and called Odette. Keeping low and beneath the line of sight of the glass on the door, he scurried up the stairs and into the bedroom.

'Pick up, Odette!' He grabbed his suitcase from the wardrobe and flung it onto the bed.

'Nik, what is it? Why aren't you asleep like the rest of the sane people of Paris?' she grumbled. 'It's four in the morning.'

'I was asleep. The police are outside.'

'What?'

'The police are here,' he hissed.

'I don't understand.'

'Nor do I.' He tossed in his clothes, covering his gun, ammunition, TASER, knife, passport, and the printouts with information on Resnik, the prime minister, the police commissioner and other politicians.

'*Mon dieu*! The number-plates on the motorbike. The detective must have traced them to your location,' she said, her words tumbling out.

'She can't have,' he said. 'I was too far away for her to see the number-plate, and you changed the cameras for the journey back here. Are you able to find out why the police were called out?'

'*Un* moment.' Her muttering entered his ear as he stashed the toiletry bag into his backpack.

'Odette? Have you found anything?'

There was no response.

'Odette?'

'It's not the police. Someone called for an ambulance.'

Nik sank down onto the edge of the bed, closed his eyes and breathed a sigh of relief. 'That's too close for my liking.' He then got up and went to the window, pulling the curtains open a fraction. He tensed. 'It's not just an ambulance, the police are here as well.' He let the curtain fall back into place.

'Let me check. From the interchange between the paramedic

and the hospital, a man fell through a window and slashed his arm and face. The police were called in just in case it was domestic violence,' Odette read out to him.

'That means the police will be back in the morning to ask neighbours if they heard or saw an argument between the couple,' he said. 'I have to leave.'

'That may be a good idea,' agreed Odette.

CHAPTER 22

Nik perched on the sofa perusing the map of Paris spread out on the coffee table. He needed a place where he could move in and out without attracting attention when he used the coin to teleport. He rang Sébastien, who told him to remain in the house and that he would be right over.

'Keep the curtains closed and do not go outside. If you turn on the television or radio, keep the volume to normal levels,' the Frenchman cautioned.

'What about the neighbours, Sébastien? They know I'm home, I've spoken to the couple next door,' Nik said. 'They will tell the police an English-speaking man is leasing the house.'

'Why are you talking to the neighbours?' asked Sébastien, incredulous.

'I was being friendly, and they were outside in the garden. It would have been rude to not say hello,' Nik replied, running his fingers through his hair.

'Okay. *Tout va bien.* Leave it to me. I have an idea.'

That conversation had taken place an hour ago.

Nik started pacing back and forth, and checking the clock on the wall. Frustrated, he moved the coffee table out of the way, and yanked off his t-shirt. He lay on the carpet and began doing sit-ups and then he went into push-ups. He was halfway through a third set of sit-ups when he heard the back door rattle. Breathing hard, Nik scrambled to his feet. He edged up to the wall of the kitchen and peered around the corner. He stared at the person waving at him through the kitchen window, the early morning orange and pink hues of the sunrise peeking behind the trees. He walked into the kitchen and opened the door.

'Elayne, what are you doing here?'

'Odette asked me to come over.'

Nik's eyes widened. 'Odette asked you ... to come here?'

She nodded. 'She couldn't leave her apartment, a water pipe in her bathroom burst and she has to wait until she can call for a plumber to fix it. Her friend Sébastien dropped me off and told me not to use the front door.' Elayne's heated gaze ran over his sweaty torso. 'You have been exercising.'

'What did Odette tell you?' he asked as he opened the fridge and grabbed a bottle of water. He offered her a drink.

'Water is fine.' Nik took out another bottle and reached for a glass in the cabinet over the sink. 'She said you needed a decoy in case the police came.'

He drank a mouthful of water. 'Aren't you needed at work?

'It's my day off.'

Nik's phone rang.

'*Bonjour*, Sébastien. Yes, Elayne is here. Can you tell me what your idea is?' Nik took another mouthful as he listened to his friend. He choked and spluttered. 'You could have warned me! I'm not sure this is a good suggestion.' He looked at Elayne. 'Are you sure about doing this?' he asked her.

'*Oui*. I agreed to help as soon as Odette mentioned you were in trouble.'

'I'll talk to you later, Sébastien.' Nik hung up and bit his lip. 'I guess we should flesh out our story.'

Her eyes lit up, and she sidled up to him, running a hand across his chest and downwards. He caught her hand.

'Elayne, this is serious. I can't afford to have the police suspect me.'

'Don't worry, Nik. By the time the police leave, I will have convinced them we're in love and devoted to each other,' she said in a seductive tone.

'You realise this is an act, a pretence?'

'Of course, but to make the police believe we're in an intimate relationship, we need to be persuasive, *oui*?' she arched a brow at him.

He sighed. 'Okay. How do we go about making our fake relationship look real?'

Elayne unbuttoned her blouse. 'We leave evidence.' Nik looked away but not before he glimpsed her cleavage and the rose-coloured lacy bra. He slugged back the rest of the water. She took his hand and led him into the living room. 'Pick up your t-shirt and take off your jeans.'

'Is that really necessary?' he asked, the blood warming in his veins.

'*Oui*. Where is the bedroom?'

Nik rubbed his sweaty palms up and down his jeans. 'Upstairs.'

She frowned. 'Why haven't you taken off your jeans?' She beckoned him with a querying look. 'I require your clothes.'

He handed her his t-shirt, and palmed the coin before removing his jeans and giving those to her as well.

'Very nice,' she beamed as he stood there in his black trunks. She swung away and sashayed towards the front of the house and dropped his t-shirt by the foot of the stairs, her blouse on the first few steps, and his jeans she flung over the railing. She slipped out of her jeans and dropped them where she stood. Her lacy pants matched her bra. She glanced over her shoulder at him, as he remained stock-still at the base of the staircase. 'Come here and undo the clip on my bra.'

'I ... um ... I ... ah ... I'm okay here.'

'Not if the police knock on the door.' She reached behind her back. 'We must be in the bedroom when they arrive.' With one swift and experienced movement, she unclasped the clip of the bra and hung it on the balustrade. Nik wiped his mouth with the back of his hand and slowly ascended the stairs. She turned around and his breathing quickened.

'Odette isn't listening in, is she?' she asked huskily.

He shook his head. 'How did you know ...'

'From your reactions yesterday.'

'Oh ...'

A loud, insistent rap at the door shattered the silence in the house.

'*Bonjour! C'est la police!*

Nik and Elayne looked at each other.

'I'll answer the door and if they ask after you, I'll tell them you're asleep,' she said as she moved to the bedroom door.

'Aren't you going to put on your clothes?' he asked frowning.

She grinned at him. 'Your shirt is enough. It will convince them of our romance.'

The police knocked again, the raps firmer and louder. Nik watched as she walked away, light on her feet like a ballet dancer, poised and confident. She pivoted, the curves of her breasts, flat stomach and hips framed in the doorway, gave him a wink and went down the stairs. A few moments later he heard the door open and Elayne greet the police. They asked her questions and though he couldn't understand every word, he worked out the gist of the conversation. Five minutes later, Elayne closed the front door and returned to the bedroom. She had collected their clothes, and handed Nik his jeans. She sat on the edge of the bed to pull on her jeans.

'What did the police ask?'

She winked at him. 'If you were available to speak to. I told them you were asleep after a very busy night and needed to rest as I have further plans for you.'

'Is that when they laughed?'

She smirked. '*Oui.*'

'What else did they ask?'

'How long you have been in the house, when we began to see each other, how we met and whether we had seen anything amiss with the couple across the road.'

Nik went cold.

'What did you tell them?'

'You have been here for about a week, that we met in the library where I work, which is true, and it was love at first sight. And we had seen little of the neighbours as we have been too preoccupied with each other.'

He stared at her.

'What is it? Did I say something wrong?' she asked, concerned.

Nik pinched the bridge of his nose. 'No, you haven't. It's just that, the neighbours know I have been here alone. If the police ask them about me, they will say they've never seen you.'

Elayne paled and spoke fast. 'We can say you've been staying at my place in the evenings, and this is the first instance you brought me to your residence.'

'We must wait and see. If the police don't return, we'll know they believed you.'

'And if they come back?' she asked, biting her lip.

Nik put an arm around her and kissed her on the forehead. 'I'm sure you were persuasive, and they may not bother to check back.'

Elayne nodded, though from the downturn of her mouth, he knew she was upset.

CHAPTER 23

Nik was sitting on the sofa, his feet propped on the coffee table with his laptop on his lap, perusing the city of Rome when Elayne emerged sleepy-eyed, wearing one of his t-shirts. She sat down next to him and yawned, skimming the screen.

'I made a fresh pot of coffee. Would you like one?' he asked her, about to get up.

She put a hand on his knee and stood. 'I will get it. Would you like another cup?' she asked, pointing at his empty espresso cup.

'*Oui.*' He smiled.

'A little more time with me and you will become a true French resident,' she joked.

'Hmm ... we'll see. There's fruit, yogurt and pastries if you would like something to eat,' he called out after her as she walked into the kitchen.

Elayne poked her head around the door. 'Is the fruit in the fridge?' Nik nodded, and she disappeared back around the corner. He heard her opening cupboard doors and taking out tableware. 'Why are you looking at the city of Rome?' she asked.

'Research,' he replied, zooming in on a section of the ancient city, writing down names of shops and their addresses on a notepad.

'Research? Maybe I can help you. After all, I am a librarian,' she said, carrying a tray with two cups of coffee, a small bowl of fruit and a plate filled with pastries. 'What is it you do when you are not eluding capture from the police?'

'I teach ancient history to high school students,' he answered.

'Really? I did an arts degree in ancient history,' she said in a cheerful tone. 'No wonder we get on so well, we have the same interests.'

Nik reached for a few grapes. 'I should be teaching my senior students, preparing them for their exams, except I'm here. Not the best timing for my students.' He glowered. 'Finding my grandfather is more important.' He reached for a cup of coffee. 'Thank you for the refill.'

'*Vous êtes les bienvenus.*' She picked up a quartered apple. 'May I ask you something?'

'Sure.'

'How much trouble are you in? I realise you cannot tell me everything, but if I can help, I would like to.'

'You've already done so much,' he said. 'Pretending to be my girlfriend for the police and assisting me in arranging the delivery of the information for the detective is more than I expected.'

'I'm not confident I convinced the police with our story,' she said with a sigh, cupping her cheek, elbow propped on the armrest of the settee.

'We will know in the next twelve to twenty-four hours.'

'Do you think they will be back that soon?'

'If a story is too good to be true, then it must be a lie.' He tossed back the remains of his coffee. 'I expect they will be back later today or early tomorrow.'

'I'm sorry, Nik. I wanted to make them believe me.' She covered her face with her hands.

'You never know, they may have.' He gave her a hug. 'It'll be okay. You can help me find a hotel close to Piazza Navona.'

CHAPTER 24

Nik was in the kitchen when Sébastien arrived later that day. He padded out into the hallway wiping his hands on the dish towel and saw Elayne descend the stairs to answer the door. She had showered, dressed in jeans, and was wearing another of his clean t-shirts that she knotted at her midriff. He bellowed a greeting to his friend and went back into the kitchen.

'*Bonjour*, Monsieur Nik,' responded Sébastien in a jolly tone. 'What are you cooking? It smells delicious.'

'It's prawns sautéed in garlic and tomatoes along with squid ink pasta,' he replied. 'Would you like to join us for dinner?'

'Hmm ... my wife may get upset if she learns I have eaten before I get home. She tells me it's important for me to be home in the early years, as things will change when they become teenagers.'

Nik nodded. 'Your wife is wise. Teenagers are not the best communicators. Adolescent boys grunt and eat everything in the pantry and refrigerator. Speaking of the fridge, would you like a beer?'

'*Oui.*'

'Elayne, would you like a glass of pinot noir?'

'*Oui, merci*, that would be lovely.'

Nik handed Sébastien a beer and poured a glass of wine for Elayne.

'*Alors*, how did my idea go yesterday?' Sébastien asked, looking from Nik to Elayne, his eyebrows raised.

Elayne's face crumpled.

'What happened?' he asked, setting his bottle down on the kitchen bench.

Nik gave Sébastien a quick rundown of the police's visit. 'It will be okay, Elayne.' He gave her a one-arm hug and she buried her face against his chest. He stroked her back.

'Ah ...' Sébastien pulled on his chin appraising them with bright eyes.

'Will you be taking Elayne home?' asked Nik.

'It will be better if Elayne remains here at least for the next few days. If the police do return, her presence will give strength to your holiday romance,' Sébastien replied tapping his lips with a finger.

'*Oui*, and I will make it right,' she said, her voice subdued.

Nik swallowed some of his beer. 'What about work?'

'I can call in for some leave, I have days owing from overtime.' She turned to Sébastien. 'I'll need fresh clothes.'

'Give me the keys to your apartment and I will have my wife pack a bag. Write down the items you require and where to find them.'

'There's a notepad and biro in the living room, on the coffee table.' Nik watched her walk into the next room, her hips swinging.

Sébastien whispered at him, his eyes as wide orbs. 'Did you and Elayne ...'

'Of course not.' Nik frowned.

'She's very attractive.' Sébastien's eyes gleamed.

'She is and easy to chat with, but I would rather not complicate our relationship,' said Nik and took another sip of his beer. 'I'd prefer to convince Detective Sauveterre that we should work together and stop all this subterfuge.'

A few minutes later, Elayne re-entered the kitchen and handed Sébastien a piece of paper. He drank the rest of his beer and pointed the bottle at Nik.

'I suggest you work on your story. I have a feeling the police will be back.' He folded the list and put it in his shirt pocket. '*Bonne nuit.* Enjoy your dinner.'

Nik saw Sébastien out, and headed back to the kitchen. Elayne was setting the table.

'I agree with Sébastien. We need a history for our relationship, and get our stories straight for the police,' he said.

She straightened. 'Shall we begin with meeting at the library and your interest in libraries and research?'

Nik nodded. 'That could work. We met a week ago when you were having lunch outside.'

Elayne walked over to him and put her arms around his waist. 'We can make our romance more convincing if we actually have an *affaire.*'

He smiled at her. 'I'm flattered, and if we'd met under different circumstances, I would be interested, but life has taken me on a different path.'

'*C'est la vie.*' Her arms dropped to her sides, and she glanced over at the stove. 'I think the pasta is ready.'

He tested the spaghetti. 'Time to eat.' Nik dished up, and they sat at the table, glasses filled with wine.

'Why must you contact Detective Sauveterre?'

'She's searching for my grandfather,' he said. 'I'm hoping the information Odette has found will convince the detective to use her resources to help me and together we look for Papou.'

'Your visit to the library two days ago was to give the detective important papers?' she asked.

He nodded. 'Intel that I hope has swayed or at least will make her a little more open to a partnership.'

She toyed with the food on her plate. 'You never answered when I asked how much trouble you are in. Is it life-threatening?'

Nik didn't answer straight away. 'There is the potential for something to go wrong,' he admitted.

'That's not what I asked,' she said, her mouth pinched.

'It will be okay, Elayne. I can take care of myself,' he reassured her.

'Have you ever been in a fight or defended yourself in an altercation?'

He wanted to tell her about his training in physical combat and using weapons, that he was more than capable of protecting himself from an attack, but couldn't do it without revealing the secret that members of his family had kept for over three thousand years. He would honour his grandfather's guardianship of the coin and not reveal his legacy even to someone as intelligent, pretty and captivating as Elayne.

'A bit of a punch-up, the usual stupid stuff guys get into,' he said with a shrug.

'Let the detective handle it!' she implored.

'I'll call the detective in the morning.' He grasped her hand. 'Her response will determine what action I take.'

CHAPTER 25

'I prefer your blue eyes. It's like gazing up into the sky. Light and very sexy,' said Elayne, coming up behind Nik in the bathroom and watching as he slipped on the brown contact lenses. 'Those contacts don't match your handsome face.'

He glanced at her in the mirror. 'As long as they work and give me the leverage to get around without being easily recognised. This will be a good test to see if they work on the police. A patrol car may turn up today. Let's go over our story once more. Where did we meet?'

'I was having lunch on the river near the library when you stopped to ask for directions to the Louvre. We struck up a conversation, and you invited me to dinner that night. You picked me up at the library at the end of my shift and afterwards while walking along the river, you asked me out for lunch the next day. You wanted to know about which places to see while in Paris and asked if I would be your guide for the duration of your stay. I said yes, of course.'

'When did we meet?'

'A week ago, and after having lunch the next day, we spent the weekend together. That was when we had our first intimate night, and have since spent most evenings with each other. Mostly at my apartment, but for the last few days I have stayed overnight at your place.' She tilted her head up at him. 'Do I get an A?'

Nik grinned, the corner of his mouth lopsided. 'An A plus.'

There was a knock at the front door. Nik threw the blanket off, got up, pulled on his jeans and t-shirt, and padded downstairs to the front door. He checked the peephole, his brows arched in surprise at the visitor.

'Odette, what brings you here?' he asked, letting her into the house. 'Did the plumber fix the leaky pipe?'

'I have tidings from your Detective Sauveterre,' Odette replied, searching the front room, up the stairs and down the passageway. 'The plumber took two days to repair the piping. He replaced not only the one with the hole but had to lay new pipes.'

'Just as well you had the plumber come when he did. Water damage would have been more expensive if you hadn't had the work done.' He led her to the back of the house and into the kitchen. 'Coffee?'

'*Oui.*' She leaned against the counter. 'Is Elayne still here?'

'Yes, she is. She's upstairs,' he replied spooning the coffee granules into the filter.

'Did the ploy work?'

'Didn't Sébastien fill you in?'

'*Non.* I've been busy with the plumber and your detective.'

Nik switched on the coffee machine and took out three cups from the overhead cupboard. 'The police came by to ask questions and Elayne did her part exceptionally, but there was a little snag with some of the finer details of our fake romance. It's been quiet since then,' and the police haven't returned. I'm hoping that's a good sign the ruse worked. What news do you have about the detective?'

'I've tracked her online searches.' Odette pulled out sheets of A4 paper from her bag and handed them to him. 'Sauveterre started researching her commander almost straight away after she received the documents you left for her. It's hard to determine if she believes what you gave her, but based on her career as a police officer, she is dedicated and seeks the truth. Learning about her commander's collusion with Resnik should create doubt.'

Nik skimmed through the notes. 'You could've rung and told me all this.'

'I thought it important to update you on what the detective's been up to. There's more Intel you can share when you speak to her, if you haven't spoken to her yet,' she said.

'No, I wanted to wait at least a few days after I gave her the information at the library before getting in touch with her. From my interactions with her, I figured she would want to investigate her boss's background.' He waved the papers at her. 'Thank you for this.' He perused the next few sheets. 'Very good Intel.'

'Good morning, Odette!' Elayne greeted her in a bright cheery tone and hugged her. 'What brings you here?'

'I had papers to give Nik,' she answered.

'And with any luck, it may change the detective's mind.' He folded the sheets in half and put them on the table. He then turned to the coffee machine.

'What happened when the police stopped by?' asked Odette.

'I'm not sure if they believed me,' replied Elayne.

'It was a simple cover story,' Odette said, her brows furrowed.

Nik handed her a cup and passed one to Elayne.

'It was, except we didn't have time to concoct a plausible story for the pretence of a holiday romance. If only you or Sébastien told me beforehand about the scheme.' He raised a finger. 'And I wouldn't have agreed to it.'

'The idea wasn't all Sébastien's, and if the pipe hadn't ruptured, perhaps the deception of an *affaire* would have gone smoother if I was here instead,' Odette stated with an indifferent shrug.

'Elayne did a wonderful job of pretending to be my girlfriend,' said Nik. 'We didn't go into enough details of the romance, though we have done now. We are prepared for when the police come back.'

'How soon do you think that will happen?' Odette queried.

Nik scratched his head. 'Who knows? They may be happy with Elayne's explanation.'

Odette sipped her coffee, her gaze flicking from him to Elayne. 'Let's hope they believed your story.'

'I think we're good,' said Nik. 'If they were going to come back, they would have done so. Then Elayne is safe to go home and back to work.'

'Are you sure? I would be happy to remain just in case,' said Elayne, looking at him.

Nik smiled. 'Thank you for your kind offer, but after I speak to the detective, and depending on the outcome, I will be leaving for Rome. This has been a pleasant sojourn and as much as I have enjoyed your company, I need to resume my search for my grandfather.' He turned to Odette. 'My sincere thanks for coming by and bringing the information, this extra leverage will help my discussions with the detective. I'll contact her shortly but I will wait until you get home before I do that, in case she runs a trace on the phone.'

Odette nodded and put the coffee cup down on the table. '*Oui*, no doubt she'll try to track your call. I will ring you when I have arrived home.'

CHAPTER 26

Nik fished out the detective's card from his wallet and sat on the edge of the bed, a thumb poised over the keypad of his phone. While he waited until he heard from Odette, he read the information she had uncovered on the detective. The Intel confirmed his deductions about Detective Sauveterre's personality, that she had been the top graduate in the police academy and her success rate in capturing criminals was outstanding. If anything, her character traits revealed how determined and motivated she was, and the extreme lengths she would take to solve a case.

The outcome of their conversation had two possibilities. In the first scenario, the detective believed the documentation on her commander and other corrupt politicians and agreed to allow him to participate in the search for his grandfather. In the second scenario, she disavowed the information. If that happened, he needed to be prepared with a strong argument for working together to change her opinion about him and his grandfather. If he could not get through to her, then he would continue to operate on his own.

He also had to consider Elayne's safety. He should have sent her home rather than go along with the pretence of a romance. He would ask Sébastien to take her home and have no further contact with her. He got up and paced the room, ordering his thoughts and what he was going to say to the detective. The screen on his phone lit up.

'*Bonjour*, Odette.'

'You are all set to go. I have re-routed your phone number.'

'The police won't be able to trace it?' he asked.

Odette snorted. '*Bien sûr que non!* If they ever do, then it's time for me to quit hacking.'

'*Merci*, Odette. You are an extraordinary woman.'

'*Je sais que*, that I know. Make your call.' She hung up.

He tapped in the phone number, the ringtone kicking in after he entered the last digit.

'*Bonjour*, Detective Sauveterre *que parle*.'

'Good day, Detective—'

'*Un moment s'il vous plaît*,' came her quick response. A myriad of conversations, the rustle of shuffling paper and ringing phones filtered through the line. Then there was a complete absence of noise. Nik banked on his judgement of her fidelity and her curiosity to learn the truth. 'Nikolaos Zosimos, I wondered when I would hear from you.'

'Have you read the documents?' he asked, curious she said 'when' and not 'if'.

'I have. The commissioner is an upstanding French citizen and has dedicated his life as a law enforcer. The information is spurious and defames an honest and outstanding officer,' she said, her tone guarded.

'You mean to say there is nothing in those papers that concerns you? Not the occasion when he intervened to stop the apprehension of the drug cartel leader Renard Larue? What about his bank accounts and the one he has in Switzerland? He has accumulated a fortune and even more wealth in his years as a commissioner than his former years as a detective,' Nik pointed out.

'You have no proof to substantiate any malfeasance,' she objected.

'It's all there. Verifiable and cross-checked, including addresses of villas and properties he owns in Nice and Switzerland. Quite the nest egg your commissioner has accumulated. Has he intervened in your case of my grandfather and Resnik?'

The line went quiet.

'As I expected. You have read of the connection between Resnik and your boss.' Nik let the card fall on the bed. 'We should work together. And after we find my grandfather, I will help you gather as much evidence and information on Resnik, Larue and your commander as you need to bring convictions against them, not to mention the politicians who are also involved.'

'Why should I trust you? You have lied to me from the beginning,' she said.

'I haven't lied, you made assumptions that were wrong.'

'You should have told me Resnik kidnapped your grandfather during our discussion.'

'I couldn't tell you. I didn't know who had taken him. I received the note after we met, and that's when I learned Resnik had abducted my grandfather. I was instructed to go to Rodin's Museum and had no time to call the police,' Nik argued.

'Was there a photo of your grandfather tied to a chair that accompanied the note?' the detective asked.

'What ... you found the photograph?'

'It was under the bed in the hotel room. In your haste to leave, you forgot the picture,' she said.

'I haven't forgotten. The image of my grandfather bound to a chair is imprinted in my memory,' he flung back. 'I don't need the photo to remind me. What I expect is an apology from you and the Interpol agent Janssens for accusing me and my grandfather of collaborating with neo-Nazis. My great-grandfather fought in the Second World War defending Crete from the Nazis.' Nik heard the stairs creak. 'You have a decision to make Detective Sauveterre.' He disconnected and tossed the phone onto the bed. Elayne appeared in the doorway, biting her lip.

'Is she going to help you?' she asked.

His shoulders sagged. 'I don't know.'

She sat next to him and took his hand. 'Perhaps she needs time to consider the information you gave her, and don't forget she is a female in a male-dominated environment. Any decision she makes, they will use it against her. If she overreacts, she will be accused of being too emotional, and if she goes in too hard, her counterparts will criticise her as being a cold, hard bitch.'

'Either way, she is hindered and culpable no matter what she does.' He clasped the back of his neck.

Elayne nodded. 'What are you going to do?'

'Wait a while and call her back,' he replied.

CHAPTER 27

Nik, Elayne and Sébastien sat at the coffee table studying a map of Paris. Sébastien had arrived not long after Nik had spoken to the detective and brought with him a bag of fresh clothes for Elayne.

'Before I call Detective Sauveterre again, I want to have a place in mind to meet her. Any recommendations?' he asked them. 'I was thinking of a location where there are lots of people, similar to Disneyland.'

'The Eiffel Tower and the Arc de Triomphe are always full of tourists,' suggested Sébastien.

'They were the two places I was thinking of,' he said, tapping the landmarks on the map with a finger.

'There is also Les Invalides and the Cathedrale Notre-Dame or the Louvre,' added Elayne.

'Which of those locations is better to blend into the crowd and disappear?'

'The Eiffel Tower and the Arc de Triomphe have the greatest number of people throughout the day, but in both it is difficult to flee unless you remain outside on the ground level,' Sébastien answered. 'It will be the same problem for the sites Elayne mentioned. Whichever one you choose, I will contact my friends, the same ones who helped us at Disneyland.'

'There are the catacombs under the Arc de Triomphe and near the Eiffel Tower,' Elayne mentioned.

'Show me,' said Nik.

She searched on her phone and pointed to the egress channels.

'Is the access to the catacombs easy to find at the Arc de Triomphe?' Nik asked her.

'There's an entrance near the underground passage that goes from Champs-Élysées to the monument.'

'I didn't know there was a way into the catacombs from beneath the Arc de Triomphe,' commented Sébastien, surprised. 'How did you learn about them?'

Elayne rolled her eyes. 'I'm a librarian, I have access to historical documents and plans of Paris since the 1300s.'

Sébastien whistled. 'That is very handy.' He looked at Nik. 'Elayne can get the information we need from old schematics—'

'No.' Nik glowered at him.

'But—'

'I said no.'

'Nik, I can help. I want to,' she said.

Nik shook his head. 'No. What you've just told me is good enough to locate the catacombs. You pretending to be my girlfriend is the extent of your involvement.'

'Okay Nik, here's what I think will work,' said Sébastien as he drew an outline of the monument on a piece of paper.

Nik and Elayne listened as Sébastien spoke, pointing to the entrances and exits sections. He drew in the famous arch, and marked Xs of his friends' positions, with backup strategies in case the meeting did not go well.

'That could work,' said Nik, appraising Sébastien's drawing. 'If

I need to use the catacombs, could one of your friends meet me at the exit with my motorbike?'

'*Oui*, I will wait there for you.'

'Great, thanks.' Nik could feel the anxiety emanating from Elayne as she sat and listened. 'Now, what day and time is the busiest to visit the Arc de Triomphe?'

'Saturday afternoon from three o'clock is the best time to go,' Sébastien replied.

Nik clasped his chin and rubbed his lips with a finger. 'Today is Wednesday. I think Saturday is too far away for a meeting. Either tomorrow or Friday.'

'Are you calling the detective again today?' asked Sébastien.

'I was going to,' replied Nik.

'Ring her tomorrow from the Arc de Triomphe and tell her to meet you there,' said Sébastien.

'That way she doesn't have time to organise a team to back her up.' Nik finished.

Sébastien nodded. 'Based on what happened at Disneyland, she was well prepared. Plus, I can contact my friends to see if they're available.'

'Right, I go tomorrow. I can't delay any further, not knowing what will happen to my grandfather the longer this situation goes on,' Nik said. 'I'll ring Odette and tell her our strategy so she can plot a route to and from the monument, and as a precaution from the catacombs.'

'Okay. It's possible not all my friends will be able to help,' said Sébastien.

'That's okay. Besides, the meeting depends on Detective Sauveterre and whether she agrees to the arrangement,' said Nik.

'Good. Another adventure,' grinned Sébastien, rubbing his hands.

Elayne barked at him in French, her eyes flashing.

'I apologise, that was thoughtless of me,' Sébastien responded in subdued tones, holding out his hands as if to ward off a physical attack. 'I shall leave,' he said, standing up.

'Perhaps you can take Elayne home?' asked Nik, getting to his feet.

Sébastien glanced at Elayne, who got up from the sofa and stormed out of the room.

'O ... kay, maybe tonight isn't the best time,' said Nik, scratching his chin.

'*Non*. And I would rather not drive with an angry woman in my vehicle.'

'Ah-huh, I will be in touch with Odette either way regarding the meet-up with the detective,' said Nik as he walked Sébastien to the door.

'*Adieu*, Nik.'

'*Adieu*, Sébastien.'

Nik found Elayne brooding in the kitchen. 'You know Sébastien's comment was innocent,' he said. 'Anyway, what did you say to him?'

'If he wants an adventure, he should go back to Disneyland and go on the rides.'

Nik laughed. 'Somehow, I don't think that's all you said.'

CHAPTER 28

'The traffic to the monument is heavier than normal,' said a distracted Odette, her voice coming over Nik's earpiece as he rode on his motorbike through the streets. 'I'll redirect you through back roads to avoid arriving late.'

'Okay, thanks Odette.'

Nik sped along Avenue Lenine, came to a roundabout, turned onto Avenue Paul-Vaillant-Couturier, and stopped at the traffic lights. Odette gave him further directions and soon he was racing along the N410.

'Do you think the detective will permit you to be involved in the search for your grandfather?' she asked.

'We'll find out soon enough,' he replied.

'You will be careful, won't you? She may arrive with backup,' Odette cautioned.

'That's possible, but giving her a brief window to meet me will be to my advantage. Do you know if Sébastien and his mates are at the Arc de Triomphe?'

'Sébastien messaged; they're in place.'

'I didn't expect Sébastien's friends to gather on such short notice.'

She snorted. 'They are reliving their glory days by playing in the shadows.'

Nik chuckled. 'Well, I'm grateful to Sébastien and his friends for helping me.'

She gave him another set of directions.

'By the way, thank you for the passport. It looks like a real one. I didn't think I would ever need a fake visa, but you obviously did,' he said.

'*Oui*, it is essential for people like you who cannot use their proper ID, to avoid detection from law enforcement agencies,' she said.

'I don't know how you do it, but I'm glad you're on my side. You are exceptional at what you do, do you know that?'

'*Oui*, I know.'

Nik chuckled again. 'I don't know how I'm ever going to repay you,' he said.

'There is nothing to repay,' she said.

He frowned. 'I can't let—'

She interrupted him. 'You are ten minutes away from the monument. There is street parking on Avenue Carnot. There's a set of stairs that will take you to the underground passage, follow the signs to the Arc de Triomphe.'

'Okay.'

He weaved in and out of the traffic, the Arc de Triomphe coming into sight.

'I have arranged your E-ticket; check your messages.'

'Will do.' He parked the motorbike.

He stared at the imposing structure, a commemorative building for Napoleon's victorious campaigns, reminiscent of Ancient Roman commanders who led their legions through triumphal arches to showcase their captured treasures and prisoners. Crowds of people amassed at the base and though not as busy as he would have liked, the gathering was large enough for him to blend in.

'Anything else I need to be aware of?'

'*Oui*, don't get caught.'

'Sage advice.'

Nik removed his helmet, secured it in under the seat and made his way to the subway entry. He squinted at the bright artificial lighting in the underground tunnel and joined other pedestrians walking in the same direction. He shoved a hand into his pocket, reassured by the presence of the coin.

He saw a familiar face, a friend of Sébastien's, who came from the opposite direction as he neared the staircase. The man scaled the stairs ahead and blended into the crowd. Nik followed a few steps behind, donning his sunglasses as he emerged near the memorial. He wandered around the Arc taking photos of the sculptures, reading the names of the soldiers carved into the interior of the walls. He skimmed the faces around him picking out a few other of Sébastien's friends and checked for plainclothes police officers. Nik lingered a little longer, satisfied, and headed for the ticket station. He noted another friend of Sébastien's trail after him.

Nik got out his phone as he shuffled behind the person queued in front of him. The line moved quickly, and he showed his ticket to the young woman at the counter. She scanned the QR code and wished him a pleasant visit. He entered the spiral staircase that scaled the two hundred plus steps to the terrace. People in front and to his rear moved at different paces, some of them lagged and panted with each step, a great many had red faces.

'*Excusez-moi*,' he said and stepped around slow-moving individuals.

At the top of the staircase he paused to take in the views of the city, turning full circle on the spot. The backdrop, a blue cloudless sky, and in the foreground, the roads intersected on the massive roundabout in which the arch sat at the centre, a majestic reminder of its historical past. Nik walked from end to end of the terrace and spotted Sébastien at one of the virtual reality kiosks. He moved to the opposite side of the terrace, his gaze flicking from one face to another. Nik clutched his mobile phone, perspiration beading on his upper lip, and wondered if Janssens would appear as he had at Disneyland.

Nik called the detective.

'Detective Sauveterre.'

'Detective, I have more information that will aid your investigation. You have thirty minutes and not a minute more to meet me at the Arc de Triomphe. Come alone.'

'Monsieur Zosimos—'

'You have twenty-nine minutes remaining.' Nik hung up.

Sébastien wandered over to where Nik stood making a show of taking pictures with his phone.

'The detective has just arrived. She appears to be alone,' Sébastien murmured, and shuffled on to take more photos.

Nik faced the other way and snapped a few shots of the mezzanine level, zooming out to get a clearer view of the area, which had become crowded in the last half hour. He recognised the detective as she brushed strands of her windswept blonde hair away from her face and took note of how she observed the people around her. When she turned in his direction, Nik lowered his mobile phone and they stared at each other. He pivoted to take photos of the avenue and tree-lined panorama.

'Monsieur Zosimos.'

'Detective Sauveterre.'

'You choose interesting places to convene,' she said, her hands clasped behind her back as she gazed across the vista.

'It's what tourists do, visit famous landmarks,' he said, lowering his phone. 'Are you alone?'

She nodded. '*Oui.*'

'Are you really?' He narrowed his eyes at her. 'At our last meeting you had a team of cops waiting for me, including Janssens. What was he doing there?'

'My commissioner and Janssens' superior insisted we work together,' she replied. 'Orders are orders.'

Nik looked around. 'If he's here, I'm gone, and you'll never hear or see me again until I've rescued my grandfather. That's when I'll go to the press to tell them exactly how the law enforcement agencies responded to his abduction.'

She scowled at him. 'I do not respond to threats.'

'I don't enjoy being accused of being a terrorist. I have provided you with solid evidence that exonerates our involvement with Resnik, that is more than enough proof to stop threatening to arrest me.'

Her jaw worked back and forth as she studied him. 'As a police officer, I must explore all avenues in cases of missing people and foreigners visiting my country,' she finally said.

'So, you're saying it's okay to suspect victims of crimes with no probable cause of guilt? Is this a strategy you use in your investigative practices?' he shot back. 'That doesn't give me any faith in your deductive reasoning or process. I thought you would be more thorough and astute.'

The detective glowered. 'I have enough information to lay charges against your grandfather, corroborated by people who witnessed him visiting certain shops. These shops are known fronts for neo-Nazis to buy and sell artefacts to raise money for weaponry.' She put her hands on her hips. 'Are you telling me it's pure coincidence your grandfather happened to go to these stores?'

He drew in a steadying breath. 'Of course your witnesses would say that. They're too scared to say otherwise, but your evidence is circumstantial. You don't have proof or an eyewitness testimony to make an arrest. You need to investigate the connection between Resnik and the neo-Nazis, and how your commissioner is involved.'

'I am,' she admitted in a quiet voice.

Nik blinked. 'Wha ... you are?'

'*Oui*. I've been examining the files you left for me and am making enquiries into the commissioner's finances. I must be careful in my communications and what search parameters I put into the police database, or I will perjure myself and be jailed for treason.'

'What have you discovered?' he asked, taken aback by her admission.

'I have confirmed what you've uncovered on Resnik's childhood and his father's association with the Schutzstaffel. As to the commissioner, his finances are the result of astute investments,' she replied.

'I bet.' He grunted. 'Was the information you read enough to create doubt to vindicate my grandfather and I from illegal connections with terrorists?'

He watched her profile as she contemplated the wide tree-lined streets and the Haussmann apartments that proliferated throughout the metropolis. 'This is a beautiful city, and I would do anything to protect it from the likes of Resnik and insurgents.' She scrutinised him, her tawny-coloured eyes glinting. 'The photo of your grandfather bound was substantial proof to demonstrate your innocence.'

He scowled. 'Jesus, you could have led with that from the start, instead of having me believe you still think we're guilty of colluding with Resnik.'

Her eyes narrowed. 'I do not answer to you. Consider yourself fortunate I came and came alone. If it were any other detective, you would be charged with obstruction and interfering with an investigation.'

Nik gritted his teeth and bent towards her. 'Circulating my face to public transport sectors, airlines and hotels implied I was a criminal. How would that look to my parents, let alone the message it gives to the school where I teach? My life could have been ruined and defamed through shoddy police work. Now you say we're innocent.' He shook his head and swore. 'You owe me and my grandfather a public apology. And why didn't you mention the photo over the phone? Why did you even agree to meet me?'

She lifted her chin. 'To ask if you would come with me now, of your own volition, into protective custody.'

'No way,' he growled.

'Resnik has extensive resources and we can keep you safe.'

'I have my own sources and we are doing a much better job than you.'

The detective stared at him. '*Comme vous le souhaitez.*' She raised a finger at him. 'Stay out of my investigation or I will arrest you for obstruction.' She turned to leave.

'Hold on a minute.' Nik grabbed her hand and felt the same electrical surge he had experienced the first time they shook hands. 'Just to confirm, does that mean I'm no longer a person of interest to the police?'

'*Oui.*'

'I can move around Paris and not get arrested?'

'*Oui.*'

'Okay, good.' He squinted at her.

She raised a brow at him. 'However, I will arrest you if you continue to interfere in my investigation.' The detective looked pointedly at his hand and he let go.

He hesitated, wrestling with a decision and then said, 'Then you may be interested to know Resnik has a new bodyguard.'

The detective's brow knitted. 'Who is he?'

'Interpol, MI5 and the CIA have been hunting this man for a number of years.'

'What else?'

'That morsel of detail is enough for you to run a check and narrow your suspects,' he said.

She drew in a deep breath. 'Monsieur Zosimos, I am not in the mood for guessing games.'

'That's all you are getting. You want more Intel like that, you let me participate in the search for my grandfather.' He stepped closer. 'What I know can aid your search.'

'*Non.*'

'Is that it? Simply "no"?' he pressed. He could smell her perfume.

'Go back to your librarian and stay out of my investigation,' she glowered.

Her reference to Elayne gave him pause. 'Right, you have made your position clear.' He spun away from her and spotted Janssens. 'Wait! What the hell is he doing here?' Nik swung back to the detective, wrapped an arm around her waist and propelled her towards a group of tourists heading inside the monument. She tried to break his grip.

'You lied about coming alone,' he hissed, his lips brushing her ear.

'I am here alone,' she retorted.

'Janssens just happened to show up at the same time, is that it?' Nik tightened his hold, his face close to hers. He quickened his pace, forcing the detective into a trot.

'Where is he?' She turned her head as Nik weaved a path

through the congested interior. 'I didn't tell him or anyone else about meeting you.'

'He must have followed you. Didn't you check for anyone tailing you?'

She twisted around. Nik faltered. He tightened his arm around her, staggering to a stop. He looked into her tawny eyes, his heart thudding.

'No-one followed me,' she said in a mild tone, leaning back.

'Janssens did.' Nik released her and dashed down the stairs.

Nik met Sébastien on the mezzanine floor, the level below the terrace. 'Janssens is here. I need to leave fast and avoid being tailed.'

'*Merde*.' Sébastien signalled to his friends, who crowded around them as they hastened down the stairs. On reaching the ground level, they broke up into pairs and dispersed in different directions like the scattering of billiard balls on a pool table. 'What happened?' the Frenchman asked as they entered the tunnel.

Nik recapped his conversation with the detective and seeing the Interpol agent.

Sébastien swore. 'She set you up. Typical police.'

'She claims she didn't tell anyone about meeting me or where she was going.'

'She must have or how did that agent know where to find you?'

'That's a good question.' Nik pursed his lips.

'Do you believe her?'

He shrugged. 'I don't know. It's possible she was telling me the truth. Doesn't matter now, she opposed our working together. Given the detective's decision and that Interpol is on my tail regardless of being exonerated by the police, I'll remain out of sight. And if it's okay with Odette, keep working with her,' Nik said.

'I will continue to assist you too.' Sébastien nodded.

'Thank you, you are a good man, Sébastien. Will your friend allow me to continue staying at the house?' he asked. 'I'm not sure for how long but I understand if I have to move out.'

'I'm sure it will be fine, but I will ask.'

When they emerged from the tunnel, the heat from the sun-warmed pavements radiated at them and the sky was clear of clouds.

'Are you able to come over tomorrow with Odette? I have an idea I want to go through with you both.'

'It will have to be after my shift.' Sébastien jiggled his car fob as he studied Nik. '*Adieu*, Nik. I'm sorry the detective was not agreeable to your plan.'

He shrugged. 'Pretty much how I predicted it would go. No more meetings, I do this on my own from here on. *Adieu*, Sébastien.'

They shook hands and parted ways.

Nik got onto his motorbike, pulled on his helmet and tapped his headset. 'Hi, Odette.'

'*Bonjour*, Nik.'

'Time to go home. Can you guide me, please?'

'*Oui*.'

CHAPTER 29

Nik had last visited Rome ten years ago, and recalled being in awe at seeing the Colosseum and the Roman Forum. The well-dressed and coiffured locals contrasted with the pollution, dingy streets, grittiness and homelessness that pervaded the ancient majesty of the Eternal City. Modern-day Rome wasn't much different from its ancient counterpart, which for Nik, gave him insight into the city's past. That and his own Greek heritage, given their family's ancestral connection with the coin, had more meaning now that he was its guardian. Another time and under different circumstances he would have liked to visit the ruins, but it was more important to confirm his deductions.

He left Paris at 5 am that morning, knowing the drive would take over fourteen hours and longer with rest periods along the way. He stopped in Mason for a break before crossing the border into Geneva and continued along the A40 into Italy, where the busy main road had multiple tunnels cut into the mountains.

The last time he had travelled to Italy was by bus. His journey into the country riding a motorbike was a different experience.

The experience was exhilarating, but with a hint of anxiety. Nik's senses were on alert, watching traffic on the left, right, ahead, and to the rear. His hands and feet moved deftly, releasing the clutch or flipping the turning signal. He depressed the front brake with his right hand to slow down, shifted his right foot on the rear brake, and with his left foot changed gears.

Nik leaned forward, spluttering from the fumes from a diesel truck ahead that doused him in a grey plume spewing from its exhaust pipe. Not wanting to get trapped behind the truck, Nik overtook, flipped up his visor and sucked in fresh air trying to rid his nostrils of the acrid smell. He couldn't help revving the engine and overtaking vehicles, the adrenaline rushing through his body with the rhythmic hum and power of the motorbike.

Odette had warned him that communication between them would be down when he entered a tunnel, and there were many tunnels before he reached the outskirts of Milan, where he pulled into a petrol station to refill. He remembered stopping for toilet breaks at petrol stations on his first trip to Europe on a Contiki tour, and his surprise at the unusual blend of supermarkets that allowed the sale of alcohol, plus an eatery or two, all in one location. It was one of the many aspects he loved about travelling.

'Odette, are you there?'

'*Oui*, I am now. Where are you?'

'I'm close to Milan.'

'*Bon*. The trip to Rome is under seven hours unless you make another stop,' she said typing away.

'I may need to, just to take a break from concentrating. The drivers in Italy are a little more competitive than your compatriots,' he said, decelerating to avoid a van, the driver not checking as he moved into Nik's lane.

'That's an apt description,' she said, a little preoccupied. 'The accommodation I've booked for you is within walking distance of Piazza Navona. It's the Argentina Residenza Style Hotel, on Via di

Torre Argentina. Use the ID I gave you, they're expecting payment on arrival.'

'That's great, Odette, *merci*.' He glanced over his shoulder before changing lanes. 'Does the road go through Milan?'

'*Non*, not unless you want to add extra hours to your trip?'

'I would rather not.'

'Tell me when and where you are stopping so I can log into the camera system,' she said.

'Will do.' He took the A50, which became the E35. 'Keep talking to me, Odette, I'm getting a little tired and distracted. Tell me more of your hacking stories? When did you start?'

'I discovered computers in my teens and learned how easy it was to break into the school's reporting database and changed grades for a few friends. I started charging other students to alter their grades.'

'Very entrepreneurial of you,' he commented. 'Did you get caught?'

'*Non*. Once I mastered hiding my digital footprint with the school program, I moved on to more challenging systems,' she answered flippantly.

'Is this how you make most of your income?' he asked.

'It helps to pay for new computers and network usage,' she replied. 'Most of my earnings come from the rent and strata fees from my apartment building.'

Nik whistled. 'You don't need to work the nine-to-five grind then.'

'*Non*. I am what you call a free agent.'

'I'm going to need a loan to pay you back,' he quipped.

'*Non*. The bastards kidnapped your grandfather in my country, and that is unacceptable. Besides, I have access to information and resources where the police do not,' Odette said.

He went quiet. 'Odette, I—'

'Enough talk, concentrate on driving and staying alive. A close friend of mine will be heartbroken if anything happens to you,' she added. 'He wouldn't say, but I know he'd be very upset.'

Nik burst out laughing. 'Tell Sébastien I miss his company too.' He indicated and slipped between a car and another motorcyclist. 'Odette, I'm pulling over at the next stop, which is ten kilometres away.'

'I'm approaching the outskirts of Rome,' he announced hours later, slowing down as the traffic grew dense.

'*Bon*. Turn right on Via Venti Settembre and continue until it becomes Via del Quirinale.' She gave him further directions until he arrived at the hotel.

'Wow,' he said, awed by the location. 'This is some accommodation you've booked me into. It's directly opposite the ruins of Pompey's forum and what's left of a temple he commissioned.'

'I thought you would like it. Use the passport I gave you,' she reminded him. 'And be British.'

A young footman came out to greet him. Nik removed his helmet.

'Good evening, *signore*. May I take your bag?'

Nik handed him his backpack. 'Good evening. Where shall I leave my bike?'

'We will park it for you in our garage. Please come this way.'

Nik followed the footman inside to a white marble desk, where an immaculately dressed woman in a blue suit gave him a practised smiled. 'Good evening, *signore*. Your name and passport, please?'

'Alexander Griffin,' replied Nik, holding out his passport.

The woman tapped away at her keyboard. 'Your assistant booked for two nights.'

He nodded. 'Is it possible to extend the booking if my work requires me to stay longer?'

She clicked away, her face pensive. 'Yes, but it will be in another room.'

'Good. That will be fine. Thank you.'

She gave him two swipe cards enclosed in a carded folder. 'You are in Room 6.' She went on to explain when the dining room was available for breakfast, asked whether he would like wake-up service and mentioned other amenities he could access.

'*Mille grazie,*' he said.

The footman showed Nik to his room. The queen-size bed was framed by a Roman arch and a north-facing window that overlooked the city and ruins.

Nik tipped the footman, who set his bag next to the desk. When the young man left, Nik placed his weapons in the safe along with his fake passport.

CHAPTER 30

After Nik had a quick shower and changed into clean clothes, he stepped out onto the street and caught sight of the forum of Pompey. He turned away from the ruins somewhat wistful and set out northwards. The concierge had given him directions to Via dei Coronari, where there were numerous stores that sold curios and vintage goods.

With map in hand, Nik crisscrossed the labyrinth of the streets. Seeing a gap between vehicles, he dashed across Corso Vittorio Emanuele II, ducked into a side street, and followed it until he came to Piazza Navona. People were out and about, taking photos of the three fountains and the obelisk at the centre of the piazza. Restaurants with colourful awnings, names blazoned across them, lined both sides of the public space, contributing to the warm ambiance of the burgeoning nightlife.

Nik rubbed the back of his neck, his skin prickling. He stopped next to the obelisk and did a casual sweep of the crowd. Not identifying anyone suspicious, he resumed walking, avoiding the maîtres'd'hôtels waving their menus at tourists, urging people to eat in their restaurant. The cobblestoned avenue and the magnificent Baroque façades loomed overhead with the centuries of history they had witnessed, but remained silent, keeping their secrets. Nik dodged groups of tourists, passed Neptune's Fountain and entered a side street. A fleeting thought crossed his mind as he wondered if his story would be added to the streets of the Eternal City.

'*Mi scusi, per favore,*' he said, skirting slow-moving pedestrians.

He encountered a few near misses, sightseers looking everywhere but where they were going, and flitted into a narrow street. Nik breathed a sigh of relief at leaving behind the rambling groups. He saw a sign pointing to a museum of an ancient stadium built by Domitian, and further ahead a street sign with the name of his destination. About to cross the road, he caught a glimpse of someone slowing and then rushing past the intersection on the other side of the street. Nik hesitated. Was he being followed?

Nik waited a few minutes to see if the woman in a grey fitted jacket and dark pants reappeared; when she didn't, he carried on to the next street approaching Via dei Coronari. There was something familiar about the woman that reminded him of the detective. It couldn't be her as she was in Paris, however the woman's appearance niggled at him.

People wandered along the compact street seemingly made for pedestrians, the odd Vespa rider and small vehicles like the Fiat Bambino. Trees in planter boxes and ivy dressed up doorways to the old buildings and added greenery to the chipped walls that had been weathered and battered over the centuries. Small restaurants with tables for two diners set up outside were interspersed between high-end clothing shops, boutiques and antique stores.

He strolled along the street and saw the antiquities shopfronts owned by Resnik were closed. He would have to return in the morning, when they opened. Nik got to the end of the street and rubbed his forehead, a headache forming. He turned and went back the way he had come and decided to eat as it had been a long time since he stopped for lunch. The concierge had recommended a local restaurant off Via dei Coronari, not too far from Piazza Navona. Veering off the busy street, he recognised the same woman in dark pants and a grey fitted jacket slip into a clothing store. He scowled and wished he had brought his gun or at least his TASER.

A few metres along Via Giuseppe Zanardelli, Nik came to the restaurant. A maître d' greeted him, ushered him inside, and sat him at a table in a corner. He ordered a bottle of mineral water and a Peroni. The server left him with a menu and went to get his drinks. Nik perused the menu and every few minutes looked up to scan the faces of people walking past the restaurant's window. The waiter placed the beer and water on the table and took his order. Nik lifted the bottle to take a drink and gawked.

'You've got to be kidding me,' he muttered, infuriated, watching the person who walked by the restaurant.

She stopped, took a few steps back and eyeballed him, then retraced her steps and entered the restaurant. At the door she spoke in fluent Italian to the maître d' and pointed at him. She walked around the tables of diners and sat opposite him. The waiter was quick to take her drink order and beamed at her with an appreciative eye.

'You're the last person I expected to see here.' Nik glared at the detective. 'How did you find me?'

'I followed you,' she answered settling back into her chair.

'All the way from Paris? That's quite the drive. Does the commissioner know where you are? After all, you are crossing jurisdictions and outside of your official capacity as a police officer,' he stated angrily. 'Why are you here? How did you track me? Are you here alone?'

Detective Sauveterre glanced at the waiter and thanked him

for the drink. 'I saw you speaking to a taxi driver who I recognised from Disneyland and traced the number-plate of his vehicle. I followed him home, where he stayed until the next day, then tailed him to a house in Saint-Denis and saw you answer the door.' She looked away for a moment. 'The following day, I saw you and the librarian.'

Nik felt the blood drain from his face.

'Don't worry, they are not in trouble. Not for the present. But I know who they are and where they live.' She helped herself to a glass of mineral water.

'Why are you here?' he grated out, his eyes narrowed.

'You didn't heed my warning and are in violation of obstructing the law,' she said.

'You don't have any legal authority in Italy,' he said, jutting out his jaw.

'That's of no consequence, I can still have you arrested.'

He sat back in his chair. 'If that were the case, I would be in jail. Why are you really here?'

She toyed with the glass. 'I have come across ... further anomalies in my investigation.'

He quirked a brow at her. 'Anomalies? I bet. Now what? You're curious about what I know and want my help?'

'You must have a lead, otherwise you wouldn't be here in Rome,' she answered. 'What—' she glanced up as the waiter appeared with Nik's food. 'What have you ordered?'

'*Pasta alla gricia*, rigatoni pasta served with crispy pork bits, black pepper, and pecorino and Romano cheese.'

She gave the overly attentive waiter her order, and he raced off to the kitchen.

'What has brought you to Rome?' she asked.

He didn't answer. Instead he pierced the pasta with his fork and put it in his mouth. He chewed, holding her gaze.

She shook her head. '*Amende*. We work together, except,' she wagged a finger at him, 'if the investigation becomes too dangerous, you are out.'

He shook his head and wiped his mouth with the napkin. The waiter returned and set down the plate in front of her, the same dish he had ordered.

'No,' he said as the waiter moved away. 'That doesn't work for me. My grandfather and my Intel.'

She frowned. 'You must be prepared for the possibility your grandfather is harmed or dead.'

Nik skewed his pasta, the fork scraping the base of the bowl. 'He's alive. Resnik won't kill him.'

CHAPTER 31

The next morning, Nik saw the detective loitering near the ruins opposite his hotel. She appeared impatient as she glanced from her watch to the hotel's entrance, her foot tapping on the pavement. He wanted to ignore her but given they were going to work together, he thought it best to be agreeable.

He went outside, observing she was dressed in the same clothes as the previous evening and straightening out her white shirt by tugging it down. 'Good morning, Detective Sauveterre.'

'*Bonjour*, Monsieur Zosimos,' she responded.

He scanned her face and noted the dark circles under her eyes. 'Where did you sleep last night?'

She crossed her arms against her chest. 'At a *pensione*.'

'Noisy, was it?'

'A small child was upset,' she replied.

'Would you like to use my bathroom to freshen up?' he asked.

'*Non*,' she responded, stiffening. 'I'm fine.'

He shrugged. 'Suit yourself. I'm about to have breakfast, if you would like to join me.'

'I prefer to begin the search for this lead of yours,' she said.

'The shops open at ten, and our mutual person of interest may appear around then.' He gestured towards the hotel.

She pulled a face. '*Tout va bien*, but I want to be there before the stores open.'

'Sure.' He led the way into the hotel, approached the restaurant manager, gave his room number and stated he had a guest joining him for breakfast. 'May we have a table near the fireplace please?'

'Of course, Signor Griffin.' Nik ignored the look of disbelief the detective gave him, waited for the manager to check his name on the list and added a notation. 'Come this way.'

The dining room was long and narrow, just wide enough for a person to move between the marine-coloured velvet chairs and a cabinet set against the wall.

'A waiter will be with you to take your drinks order. If you prefer a hot breakfast, let your waiter know. Our buffet has fresh fruit, juices, cured ham, preserves, bread and cereals.' The manager pointed to the cabinet.

'*Grazie*,' said Nik.

The detective waited until they were alone and said, 'You are committing fraud, Monsieur Zosimos.'

'What choice did I have with you and Janssens intent on arresting me? If you want my information, this is how it's going to be, otherwise there is the door.' Nik stared at her.

Her eyes glinted. 'Does this lead have a name?'

'Wilhelm Ritterbusch. His grandfather was an SS officer and in charge of one of the concentration camps in Bavaria. Wilhelm would have grown up hearing stories about how his grandfather was prosecuted for the atrocities he inflicted on the Jewish people, and how he was wrongly accused of war crimes. White supremacist rhetoric that continued into his teens, which led him to Resnik and his so-called ideals for a superior race.' Nik paused when a waiter came to their table and took their order. 'Did he not come up as a person of interest when you did your search after our meeting?'

'He did. I wanted to confirm he was the same person you referred to as Resnik's new lieutenant.' She paused. 'How do you know he's coming to Rome and to an antique store on Via dei Coronari?' she asked.

'As you and your colleague Janssens know, many antique stores are neo-Nazi fronts owned by Resnik under a shell company.'

'And he owns one here in Rome?'

'He owns two. Resnik's been buying antique stores that sell rare coins.'

She frowned. 'How do you know for certain Ritterbusch will come to Rome?'

'Resnik is searching for something, and by purchasing these stores he hopes to find what he's looking for,' Nik answered.

She tilted her head at him. 'You know what he wants, don't you? It is what your grandfather was seeking before being abducted.'

'In a way,' he said, hesitant.

She glowered at him. 'You either be honest with me or this partnership will never work. What is Resnik after?'

'Have you ever heard of the Spear of Destiny? The Roman spear that was used to kill Jesus while he was on the cross, and how the Roman centurion who stabbed him miraculously had his poor eyesight restored?' he asked.

She nodded. '*Oui.*'

'Legend has it that Herod the Great, Constantine, Justinian and Charlemagne, to name some historical figures, had possessed the Spear of Destiny throughout their campaigns and were victorious. Napoleon wanted the spear for his invasions, but persons unknown smuggled the lance out of Austria. In the last century, the tip of the spear was returned to Austria and has since been in the Hofburg museum in Vienna. This attracted the attention of a young Adolf Hitler. The story goes that any person who seized the spear won glorious victories, which is why Hitler wanted it. Resnik is after something similar, a powerful object that will enable him to succeed where Hitler failed.' The shape of the coin pressed into his thigh.

'He is seeking a supernatural object of untold power?' she scoffed.

'Yes. And it's possible he has one-half of the object,' Nik replied.

'But you are uncertain?'

Nik wavered. 'I'm almost one hundred per cent sure he does. It's the second half he is after.'

'If he finds the other half, what would it mean?'

'I don't know, but nothing good.'

'You said he's buying antique stores that specialise in coins.'

He nodded.

'He's looking for a coin. How old?'

'Seventh century BCE.'

She stared at him, her face tightening in realisation. 'That's the story you told me when your grandfather disappeared.'

'I did, and it wasn't a story.'

Her brows knitted. 'Why this coin? What makes it so special that Resnik wants it?'

'That's what I'm trying to figure out.'

'Do you know which antique stores Ritterbusch intends to go to?' she asked.

He nodded. 'The shops are on Via dei Coronari. Two are close to each other, and a third potential store is at the end of the street.'

'That's what you were doing last evening, checking the stores.'

'I knew it was you who was tailing me.' He gripped the teaspoon he held in his hand.

She shrugged. 'And I knew you would be pursuing some clue even though I instructed you not to interfere.'

'Yet, here you are.'

The detective drew in a deep breath before asking, 'Why did you agree to meet Resnik?'

'He abducted my grandfather. You saw the photo, you would have done the same.'

'Fleeing from the police was not the smartest action to take,' she reproached him. 'You became a suspect by running away.'

'You didn't believe me anyway. Not even when I tried to explain,' he rebuffed.

'I was doing my job,' she snapped back. 'I must investigate all possibilities and probable avenues of criminal activities.'

He snorted. 'What bulldust. It was easier to implicate me rather than interrogate Resnik.'

She crossed her arms against her chest. 'I was right to come after you. You know more than what you told me at our first meeting, and I was correct that your grandfather was involved in what Resnik wants even though there may be no collusion between the two men. What is much more interesting is the story of two Australians who came to France on the pretence of a holiday. What is your interest in this coin, and why is it so important to you, your grandfather and Resnik?'

'I will let you know once I work out what the connection is,' he said.

'What was that word you used ... bulldust,' she hurled at him.

Nik wiped his mouth with the napkin and stood. 'Time to check if Ritterbusch shows up.'

CHAPTER 32

The trek from the hotel to Via dei Coronari took a little longer than Nik wished, as he had to shorten his longer stride to match that of his companion's. Walking alongside the detective instead of being pursued by her felt weird. On his return to the hotel the previous night, Nik had rung Odette and Sébastien to fill them in on the detective's presence in Rome. Their responses were not what he expected, given how they had implored him to hand over the search to the detective. They were vociferous and incensed by her unscrupulous tactics to track him.

He placated them by explaining that the detective had no intention of arresting Sébastien or Elayne for their involvement in assisting him. Thirty minutes later, he contacted his parents to let them know what was happening, except he didn't include he was involved in the police investigation. He didn't want to add to their worry, as they had enough on their plates dealing with the foreign office in Australia, which was liaising with the French officials on their behalf in the ongoing search for Papou.

'What does Ritterbusch look like?' asked the detective, disrupting his musings.

'Tall, about my height, muscular build, blond hair in a buzz cut, a tattoo on his neck, though I couldn't see what it was.' He pointed to the left side of his own neck. 'A square jaw with a deep-set brow and blue eyes.'

She grimaced. 'He is the bloodline Hitler wanted to create within the German race.'

'Yes, and he almost succeeded.'

They were about to cross the main road when Nik put an arm out as a rider on a motorbike sped past.

'I should arrest that idiot for dangerous driving!' she exclaimed, scowling down the road where the driver zoomed in and out of the traffic.

'I don't think it would matter too much to him or her,' he said with a slight smile on his face.

She gave a pointed look at the arm he had put around her waist.

'Sorry.' He stepped away and turned his attention to the road. 'We can cross now.'

A few minutes away from the piazza, Nik's ears twitched as the sound of voices grew louder. He grumbled under his breath and slowed his pace as they approached the congested forum.

'It's much busier than last night.' He side-stepped to avoid an enthusiastic photographer. 'I suggest we cut to the closest street to keep from getting held up in this crowd.'

Brightly coloured umbrellas held by tourist guides dotted both sides of the plaza, encircled by their groups of sightseers. Adults, some with children clinging to their hands, teenagers standing apart, and older people. Everywhere people were taking photos with their phones, of the fountains and obelisk.

Detective Sauveterre nodded. '*D'accord.*'

They negotiated their way through the crowd and headed onto

Via di Sant'Agnese in Agone, turned right and walked north towards their destination, the same path Nik had taken the previous evening. Before long they entered the narrow street. It too was busy with holidaymakers walking in and out of stores, cafés, restaurants and hotels.

'The first two antique stores are not too far.' He pointed. 'Just up the street. The third one is further along.'

'What if he doesn't come today?' she asked, her attention focused on the way ahead.

'We return tomorrow,' he replied.

'You're positive he's going to show up today?'

'No, I can't say he will. What I do know is he is due to visit the stores,' he answered as he examined the faces of the men in the street.

'Which is the next location, if we don't see him here?'

'Madrid.'

'I would like to know how you came across this information and how accurate it is,' she queried.

'The source is reputable.'

'From a contact?'

'Yes,' he replied, reading the names of the stores on the fascia. Nik strode ahead before he realised she wasn't alongside him. He turned, puzzled, seeing her tapping a foot once again. 'Now what?' he asked her.

'You are being evasive in your answers. Unless you're honest with me, this partnership is not going to work,' she answered irritably.

Nik tilted his head to one side. 'Fine with me.' He spun around and started back up the street, and smiled to himself when he heard her swear in French.

'Are you always this difficult?' she snapped, coming up behind him.

'Are you always this petulant?' he flung back.

'*Oui*, with people who are secretive and deceptive,' she replied simmering. She shoved her hands into her jacket pockets.

He swung round, forcing her to take a step back, his voice deepened, tone low. 'To be clear, you followed me here after telling me you didn't want to work with me. You had little information until I gave you the Intel. Where I receive my clues and who from, remains my source. Besides, you're not forthcoming or willing to share evidence and findings regarding my grandfather or Resnik.'

Nik frowned at her for a second longer before turning back and stumbling over an old woman who had hobbled out of a nearby shop. 'Oh, *scusi*.'

The woman grabbed his hand and clicked her tongue at him in disapproval. She spoke to him in Italian, pointing at the detective and then at him. Nik held up a hand and tried to extricate himself from her clutches, but the woman kept berating him. He recognised a few words and shook his head.

'No ... no ... not *amore*.'

Undeterred by his protestations, the old woman dragged him back to the detective, insistent, and demonstrated what he needed to do. His ears grew hot.

'No. We are ... colleagues.'

The detective intervened in Italian. She was expansive, waving her hands at him and herself. The old woman cocked her head at them, folding her arms over her stomach. She shook her head and responded in an amicable tone, her eyes sparkling as she looked Nik up and down and winked at the detective. She patted Nik's cheek, added a few more words and ambled down the street. Nik stared after her, dumbfounded.

'What did she say?' he asked the detective. He glanced at her when she didn't reply and saw her face was flushed.

'If she were a few years younger, she would make a play for

you. I told her you have a girlfriend back in Paris,' she said, brushing past him.

'Ah-huh ...' Nik scratched his head, bemused by the old woman's behaviour and the detective's peculiar reaction. He shrugged off the weird encounter and caught up with her. They soon came within metres of the antique stores. 'Best if we split up,' he said. 'You remain here and I'll go ahead to the other shop.'

'*Non*. We go together. You know what he's looking for,' she said.

'Fine. We'll go to the store furthest away and make our way back here.' He shrugged, trying not to show his annoyance and continued up the road.

The antique store was near an intersection. Nik pushed open the door and stood aside for the detective to enter.

She gave him a surprised look and murmured, '*Merci*.'

Nik followed her in and smiled at the well-dressed woman behind the counter. '*Buongiorno, signora*.'

'*Buongiorno*. English?' she asked, and he nodded. 'How can I help you?'

'I was wondering if you have a collection of old coins?'

'*Si*, not many. Would you like to see?'

'*Si, per favore*.'

She pulled a key from the chain around her neck to unlock the cabinet beneath the counter and pull out a tray of coins. She placed it on the countertop. Nik examined the coins and knew straight away they weren't from the right era.

'Sorry, they are not what I'm looking for. *Tante grazie*.' He turned to the detective. 'We can leave.'

The door to the store opened and Nik glanced over, blinking in the sunlight streaming through. He put an arm around the detective's waist and ushered her to the doorway, acknowledged the newcomer with a nod and stepped outside. The detective twisted away from his embrace but seeing the look on his face she peered around him.

'Wait, isn't that Ritterbusch?' she said. 'We should go back inside and question him.' She pushed at him to turn back. He held her fast and propelled them further away from the store.

'Yes, it is, and no. If you question him, we'll never find where my grandfather is being held.' He let his arm fall to his side and lengthened his stride, forcing her into a half run to keep up.

CHAPTER 33

'There's a bar and a restaurant not far from the other two antique stores,' Nik said. 'If we get a table outside at either of them, we can see Ritterbusch when he comes this way.'

'This is not how I operate,' said the detective. 'He's a key to finding Resnik and your grandfather. If I apprehend him, we are closer to learning what Resnik intends to do and to getting your grandfather back.'

'If you do that, he'll clam up. Someone like Ritterbusch will not give up information easily, and then we'll have nothing. Besides, you don't have any legal authority outside of France, that is unless Janssens is hiding somewhere.' He looked at her. 'You are here on your own?'

'*Oui.*'

He peered at her face for a moment and kept walking.

'Don't you want to see if the other stores have the coin Ritterbusch is searching for?' she asked after a number of minutes.

'His reaction should tell us if he's successful.'

Nik put a hand to her lower back and steered her through the busy street. He saw an empty table outside a restaurant that overlooked a small piazza. He pulled a chair out for the detective and sat opposite her. He had a clear view of the street. A waitress emerged and gave Nik a warm welcoming smile.

'What would you like to drink?' he asked the detective.

'*Cafe lungo, per favore*,' she said to the waitress, whose sole attention was on Nik.

'*Due cafe lungo, e una bottiglia de aqua minerale, per favore*,' he said to the waitress with a slight smile.

'*Va bene*.' She gave him a lingering coquettish look and disappeared into the restaurant with their order.

'Is this a regular occurrence for you?' asked the detective, peeved.

'Is what a regular occurrence?' he asked, confused.

The detective indicated to the waitress who was hovering at the bar and giving Nik furtive glances. 'The way women behave around you.'

He gave her a blank look. 'What do you mean?'

The waitress returned with their drinks. Nik thanked her and gave her a tip with payment of the bill. She beamed at him, her hand touching his as she took the money from him, and then sashayed away.

The detective sniffed, irritated. 'I'm surprised she didn't give you her phone number. There was the old Italian woman who made a suggestive proposition, and what of the librarian from Bibliotheque Francois-Mitterrand? Are you not dating her? What would she have to say about these women who're throwing themselves at you?'

Nik quirked an eyebrow, amused. 'Are you accusing me of being a philanderer?'

'*Non*, just ...' She shook her head and motioned with her hand. '*Peu importe*.'

'If you say so. Except there's nothing between myself and

Elayne, the librarian. She's a friend,' he added, sipping his coffee and holding her gaze.

They fell silent and Nik shifted his attention to watch the pedestrian traffic. He was opening the bottle of mineral water when he saw Ritterbusch saunter down the road. Surprising Alexandrie, he put a hand behind her head and kissed her, while keeping his eyes on the German. Her mouth yielded under his and began to respond. Nik became distracted by the softness of her lips and thrust his tongue into her mouth, probing. She dragged her mouth away.

'*Que faites-vous?* What are you doing?' she hissed, indignant.

Nik gulped back a breath. 'Ritterbusch.' He tipped his head in the direction of the tall German who was entering the antique store a little away from their position.

'Did you really need to kiss me?' she asked, slamming back in her chair.

'That's what couples do when they're on holiday,' he said, his heart racing. 'He may have recognised us from the antique store, and I thought it a good idea to avoid his attention.'

'Don't do that again!' she spluttered.

'We need a cover for being here, what better than two people snogging?'

'He could have walked by and not noticed us at all,' she growled, her eyes flashing.

He sat back in his chair and looked away from her angry face, her vehemence radiating in waves. 'Good point. I hadn't considered that.' He cleared his throat. 'Don't worry, it won't happen again.' He gulped down the rest of his coffee.

He tried to ignore her heated wrath, and wished for the German to exit the store or for the ground to swallow him. The waitress returned and asked if they wanted something else. Nik, grateful for her presence, ordered a beer. He turned to the detective, who shook her head, and noted the look of scorn on the waitress's face before she walked away. He resumed watching the store, his fingers tapping on the tabletop in time to the music that flowed out of the restaurant, unable to concentrate, recalling how the detective responded again to being kissed and the taste of her mouth. The waitress came back with his beer and laid a folded piece of paper in front of him.

'*Grazie*,' he looked up and handed her money. '*Mantenere il cambiamento.*'

The young woman tapped a finger on the paper and walked away, her hips swinging. He picked it up and put in his pocket, ignoring the look of incredulity the detective gave him. He took a mouthful of the cold lager and saw Ritterbusch leave the store and enter the shop next door. Nik's leg bounced up and down and he felt the light touch of the detective's hand on his knee. His skin tingled, his blood warming, and bit his lip.

'Be still,' she said. 'Surveillance is about waiting and patience.' She removed her hand.

Nik stretched his neck, ran a finger around the collar of his shirt and chugged back his beer, the linger of her touch sending vibrations to his loins. With a grateful sigh, he saw the German exit and pause on the store's threshold, his face showing his displeasure. He reached into his pocket, pulled out a pack of cigarettes, lit one and set off eastwards.

Nik moved to stand.

'*Attendez un moment*,' the detective murmured, her hand back on his knee.

'He'll get too far away for us to tail him if we don't move,' Nik said, impatient to get up.

'We don't want him to suspect he's being followed, we wait a few more minutes,' she said, her attention not wavering from the receding figure of the German.

Nik sat coiled like a tight spring, watching Ritterbusch walk further and further down the street.

'Now we go,' she said, standing and setting off after their suspect.

'About time,' Nik muttered.

They kept their distance as they followed him. The German turned into a street on the right. Nik and the detective slowed as they neared the thoroughfare.

'Why don't you go down the next side road and I'll take this one?' Nik suggested, peering around the corner and trying to ignore the scent of her perfume as she stood close to him.

'We stay together,' she said.

'As you wish,' he said.

When they next caught sight of him, Ritterbusch was midway down the street. Instead of continuing across the intersection, the German turned left and vanished from sight. Nik and the detective hurried to catch up and saw him enter a Baroque-style church. They pursued him inside, crossing a semi-rounded portico featuring eight Doric columns that led into a rectangular room. A door at the far end led them into an octagonal, domed space. Within was a small nave, featuring colourful frescos of angels and the holy family. In the main section of the church behind the altar above the sacristy, was a leaded glass window connecting the dome and nave.

Ritterbusch was nowhere to be seen.

Next door to the church was an art museum, both buildings sharing entries and exits. Nik and the detective exited the church through a doorway and stepped out into an open courtyard. Nik looked up towards the first floor, twisting left to right, and spotted Ritterbusch ambling along the colonnade. The German turned his head, and Nik dragged the detective under the arched walkway. He darted to the staircase, the coin in his pocket warming and pulsating.

'Nikolaos! Wait!' cautioned the detective.

Nik reached the upper level and saw Ritterbusch approach a

door on the other side of the building. He lengthened his stride, peering into windows as he walked in the pretence of being interested in what was on display. When Ritterbusch went through the door Nik ran, skidding on the stone floor worn smooth over centuries of use. He grabbed the brass doorknob and yanked the door open. White light flooded the room, and a mini typhoon propelled him backwards into the colonnade, flinging him against the stone wall. He teetered over the balustrade, arms flailing in the air. Someone grabbed him by the legs and wrenched him to safety. He fell sideways, his head hitting the ground. Darkness clouded his vision.

'Nikolaos! Nikolaos, can you hear me?' The detective was shouting.

Nik groaned, his mouth watering, the bitter taste of bile rising. 'I think I'm going to be sick.'

He rolled onto his side and vomited as the detective stepped out of the way. He collapsed against the wall and wiped his mouth with the back of his hand that shook like an earth tremor.

'What happened? Did you see Ritterbusch? What was that light and quaking?' asked the detective, squatting next to him.

'There was some kind of explosion,' he said as he tried to stand. She put a hand against his chest to stop him getting up.

'Let me check if you have any broken bones. I think you may have suffered a concussion after slamming into the wall and hitting your head on the floor,' she said, her voice tinged with concern. She ran her hands over his limbs and bit her lip when she touched his face. 'You have a fever. I'm calling an ambulance and then I'll check if anyone else was injured in the blast.'

He caught her hand. 'No, don't ring for an ambulance. They'll have to report it to the police, who will ask lots of questions.'

'I must, it's my responsibility as an officer of the law,' she said with a frown.

'How are you going to explain what you're doing here and

what happened?' He blinked and wiped his brow with the back of his hand, feeling hot. His mind was fuzzy, he was finding it difficult to keep focus. He blinked again, his vision blurring.

'I believe a detective and her boyfriend, a teacher of history, holidaying in Rome is not out of the ordinary,' she replied. 'No arguments, you need medical attention.'

A small crowd of tourists formed around Nik and the detective, the sound of sirens getting louder as an ambulance drew closer. The detective went to inspect the room where Ritterbusch had disappeared. Nik grimaced as he tried to sit up, his head swimming, and passed out.

CHAPTER 34

Nik's nose twitched as he inhaled the scent of antiseptic and the hint of bleach. His ears perked at the constant beeping of a machine. He stirred, his head thumping, reminding him of the occasions when he teleported. He opened his eyes, the disinfectant smell much stronger and the noise amplified. He looked around and realised he was in a hospital bed. Beyond the door of the ward he shared with five other people, he saw the detective talking to two uniformed police. She moved, pointing, seeing him awake. The police officers looked across and made a comment to the detective before they entered the room.

The detective walked with quick strides, keeping ahead of the officers. She took his hand, leaned down as if to kiss him on the cheek and whispered in his ear. 'We are here on a holiday, and being a teacher of ancient history, Rome was on your list of things to see.' Her lips brushed against his ear, the warmth of her breath and lavender perfume awoke every nerve in his body, his heartbeat quickened. '*Oui?*'

'*Oui,*' he replied in a hoarse voice.

She straightened, reached for the buttons to elevate the bed and perched on the side of the bed holding his hand.

'Signor Griffin, we are sorry you were in an accident in our city,' said one of the police officers.

'Thank you,' Nik said, remembering to use his cover of a British citizen.

'Can you recall what happened?'

'I was on the first floor of the gallery and about to enter a room,' he rasped. The detective gave him a cup of water and he took a sip. 'There was a flash of white light and a burst of wind. I came to when I hit the wall, with the det—' she squeezed his hand, 'Alexandrie fussing over me. Was it some detonation? Was anyone else hurt?'

'Our forensic team is analysing the scene but so far there's no evidence of a bomb and no-one else was injured,' answered the second officer.

'Can you keep me informed of what you find?' the detective asked them.

'As a professional courtesy, *si*, but understand we cannot divulge all that we uncover,' the officer replied, his tone wary.

'*Oui*, but the blast almost killed my boyfriend. Surely as a show of congeniality between law enforcers you can keep me apprised of your investigation,' she said, holding out her business card.

The police officers glanced at each other.

One of officers reached out to take the card. 'We will contact you with our results.'

'*Grazie.*' She smiled with a nod.

'How long are you staying in Rome?' the Carabiniere asked.

'We're meant to leave tomorrow,' Nik replied.

'Where are you staying?' the other queried.

'At the Argentina Residenza Style Hotel.'

'*Va bene.* I suggest you stay on a few more days, we may need to ask further questions,' said the police officer, flipping shut his notepad.

The two officers left. The detective waited until they were out of sight before she let go of Nik's hand.

'What did you see in the room?' he asked her. 'Was Ritterbusch there?'

She shook her head. '*Non*, he wasn't. He vanished. I cannot determine how as there was no other way out except through the door he entered or walking through the entire building. There appeared to be signs of an explosion. Paintings hung askew from the wall and some had smashed to the ground, some sculptures and vases were broken.' Her brow knitted as she tapped her lip with a finger and tilted her head. 'I've had a great deal of experience with bombings, and there was no evidence of remnants from an explosive device. It was clean. Very odd.'

Nik knew how Ritterbusch had disappeared but would not reveal that tidbit of information. What had surprised him were the after-effects from Ritterbusch's teleportation. He thought the impact of the side effects from the time jump were internal manifestations when he used the coin but this unusual development was something he needed to think through. The connection and close proximity between the coins had a greater consequence to himself, Ritterbusch and everyone nearby. He threw off the blanket.

'What are you doing?' she said, alarmed.

'Leaving. I'm fine. Where are my clothes?' He swung his legs over the side of the bed and swayed from side to side.

'You're not going anywhere,' she said, forestalling him with a hand on his chest. 'You have a mild concussion. The doctor wants to keep you in overnight.'

'No.' He shuffled to the edge of the bed. She didn't budge. 'I have to leave.'

He pushed off the bed and teetered. She caught him, her arms going around his waist. Nik held onto her to steady himself. He shut his eyes while he waited for the pendulum to stop. Minutes passed and he became aware of her body against his.

'Ah ... thanks.' He let go, his hands falling to the edge of the bed and sat down again.

'I'll go to the nurses' station to get the doctor,' she said, avoiding looking at him.

'Okay.' He studied the green-tiled floor. He lifted his head only when he saw her feet move away. A man in his mid-forties in the bed next to him grinned and winked at him.

'She is beautiful,' he commented, speaking in halting English. 'She stays all time you sleep. Very worried. Your wife?'

'No.'

The man raised his brows at him. '*Perché* no? You must. Before another man *la sposa*.'

'We're just ... friends,' Nik said.

'Sure, sure,' the man said scratching his jaw. 'Move quick, or she go.'

'It's not that sort of—' he stopped. The detective was returning.

She stood at the foot of the bed. 'The doctor is doing her rounds and will be here in the next twenty minutes. A nurse is coming to check your blood pressure.' She glanced at the man in the next bed. 'I see you've made a friend.'

'Talkative chap,' Nik said.

A redheaded nurse bustled into the ward, heading straight for Nik's bed. She forced the detective out of the way as she picked up the clipboard from the end of the bed. She set it down on the mobile table and tut-tutted at Nik, patting his hand, speaking in Italian and gesturing, suggesting he should be lying in bed and not sitting up. With reluctance, he reclined back against the pillows, and she straightened the bed linen over him. She popped a thermometer into his mouth, seized his wrist and checked the small fob watch pinned to her chest. She picked up the clipboard and scribbled down some notes. The nurse reached across Nik, pressing her breasts against him to pull out the blood pressure monitor unit affixed to the wall behind the head of the bed. He drew back further into the pillows and the nurse moved with him. She straightened and wrapped the cuff around his bicep, her hand lingering on his arm, her eyes widening in appreciation.

Nik noticed the detective had moved to the other side of the bed, her arms crossed. She glared at the nurse, who gave her an impassive look. From the corner of his eye, Nik spied his bedside neighbour flicking his hand up and down in front of his chest, his mouth pursed as if to whistle, and shaking his head with slow sweeps from side to side. The nurse completed her examination, patted his thigh and left the ward. Nik pressed his lips together and did not utter a word.

'Mamma mia,' murmured his fellow ward occupant.

Nik kept his gaze on his hands. If it was someone else with him other than the detective, he would have quipped and made light of the nurse's flirtatious ministrations. He didn't need to add to Alexandrie's assessment of his being a lady's man. Her reaction to the nurse's behaviour was unusual, and he wasn't sure what to say to break the awkwardness between them. He glanced across to the other man, whose eyes sparkled as he indicated to Nik to kiss the detective. A newcomer entered the ward, and he sighed with relief.

'*Buongiorno*, I am Doctor Raimondi.'

The doctor was an elegant, businesslike woman in her early fifties with short grey hair. She picked up the clipboard and skimmed through the details on the chart.

'I understand you wish to leave,' she said to Nik.

'Yes. I'm feeling much better.'

'You were unconscious for several minutes and were passed

out when the paramedics attended. You also have soft tissue damage to your upper body, the bruising had emerged when I examined you on arrival,' she stated, eyeing him. She pulled out a small torch from her pocket. 'I want to test your pupil reaction. Look straight ahead.' She waved the torch into his eyes. 'Look to the left ... look right ... up ... down.' She dropped the torch back into her pocket and raised her hand. 'Follow my finger.' She wrote down a few notes. 'I would prefer if you remained in hospital overnight but you are young and fit, you will recover.'

She turned to the detective. 'I understand you and Signor Griffin are here together on a holiday.'

'*Oui*, we are.'

'I have also been told that you are a detective from Paris.' Alexandrie nodded and the doctor continued. 'He is not to be left alone for the next twelve to twenty-four hours. Any signs of slurred speech, confusion, instability or sluggish movements, you must return Signor Griffin to hospital right away.' The doctor paused and added, 'And no physical exertions of any sort.'

The detective's cheeks flushed, and Nik looked the other way, his ears burning.

'Any other symptoms I must be aware of?' Alexandrie asked the doctor, her tone clipped.

'If light bothers Signor Griffin or if he experiences pressure in his head, he must be admitted to hospital straightaway,' the doctor replied. 'I will sign the discharge papers, Signor Griffin, and release you into the care of your girlfriend. I will have the nurse assist you to get dressed.'

'No!' exclaimed Nik and the detective in unison.

The doctor stared at them, her brows raised.

'Alexandrie can help me.' The words flew out of Nik's mouth.

'*Oui*, I'm sure the nurse is busy attending to other patients. I'll help Nikolaos change into his clothes.' The detective's eyes glinted.

'*Naturalmente*,' nodded the doctor. 'I will leave a script for Signor Griffin's medication at the nurses' station. It will help with the pain over the next twenty-four to thirty-six hours.'

CHAPTER 35

The taxi journey to the hotel was quiet. Nik watched the view outside the window as they drove over the Tiber River, the driver merging with other traffic on Corso Vittorio Emanuele II. Nik rubbed his forehead, leaned his head back and closed his eyes. Ten minutes into the trip, he opened his eyes and looked around.

'Where are we going?'

'I need to pick up my bag from the *pensione* where I'm staying,' the detective answered.

'Oh ... right.' He reclined his head again, eyelids heavy.

'How are you feeling?' she asked.

'Tired.'

'Are you in pain?'

'I have a bit of a headache.'

He listened as she spoke to the driver and felt the car pick up speed. The vehicle came to a stop twenty minutes later.

'I'll be right back, Nikolaos.'

'Okay.' He gave her a thumbs-up, his eyes still shut.

A little later, Nik checked his watch, glanced outside to see the detective returning with an overnight case in hand. He closed his eyes again, unable to keep them open. The weight of the car shifted and he sensed the detective sit back next to him. The last thing he heard was the detective giving the driver the name of the hotel.

'Nikolaos.' Someone called at him. 'Nikolaos, wake up. We've arrived at the hotel.'

He blinked, drawing in her familiar scent of lavender. It took him a moment to realise he had fallen asleep on the detective's shoulder. He roused with a start and winced, clenching his hands as a shooting pain sent spasms through his neck, shoulders and lower back. He sucked in a breath and pulled himself upright, his forehead beading with perspiration.

'I'm taking you back to the hospital,' she said, her brow puckered.

'No,' he ground out between clenched teeth. After a few moments, he began to breathe easier. 'I'll be fine once I've taken the painkillers and showered.'

The footman hurried out and opened the taxi door.

'Signor Griffin! We heard what happened. Please, let me help you.' The young man reached in and assisted Nik out of the car.

'*Uno momento*,' he murmured, stretching his neck from side to side. 'Thank you, I should be okay to walk on my own.'

'*Si*, Signor Griffin.' The footman turned to the detective. '*Buongiorno*, signorina. If it pleases you, I will take your bag.'

'*Grazie*.'

Nik made a slow walk into the hotel. The same woman who had checked him in, saw him and rushed over.

'Signor Griffin, we are so sorry to hear what happened. Anything you need, please let us know,' she said.

'*Mille grazie*, signorina. It appears I will be staying longer than the few nights I have booked,' he told her with an attempt at a grin.

'Of course, I'll make the arrangements. You will not need to move rooms.' Her eyes flicked to the detective. 'Will your friend be staying with you?'

'Yes.'

'Very good. Again, we are sorry to hear what happened and hope you recover soon,' she said. 'Anything you need, please call reception.'

'Thank you.'

Nik, Alexandrie and the footman walked to the room, the young man opening the door for Nik and setting the detective's bag down by the lounge. Nik went to tip him, but she was quicker. He sank onto the couch as the door closed, leaving them alone. The detective glanced around the room.

'I don't think I should have sat down,' he groaned, trying to get back up. The detective came to his side and helped him to his feet.

'Thank you, detective.'

'You should call me Alexandrie,' she suggested.

'Right. Alexandrie, thank you. Where are those painkillers?'

She reached into her jacket pocket for the bottle and read the directions. 'You are going to need to eat food before taking these tablets.'

'Right. Please order room service. I'm going to have a shower.'

He shuffled into the bedroom and slid the door closed. He shrugged out of his jacket and dropped it on the bed and went to pull the t-shirt over his head. Sinking down onto the bed, he tried again and struggled to lift his arms past his shoulders.

'Alexandrie? I need a little help.'

She slid open the door. 'What is it?'

He exhaled in exasperation. 'I can't take my shirt off. I'm unable to lift my arms from the pain.'

She hesitated. '*Droite*. Okay.' Alexandrie stepped into the room, took his arm, and eased it through the sleeve. He grunted, her nearness shifting his mind from the pain, until she lifted his other arm. He flinched. 'Are you okay?' she asked in a soft voice.

'Yes,' he groaned, his entire body aching. 'Wait a moment. I need to catch my breath.' He inhaled and exhaled, and again a few more times. 'Okay, I'm ready.'

She pulled his t-shirt from the waist and inched it upwards until his arms and shoulders were clear. He sagged in relief. She guided the top over his head and slipped it over his face. They gazed at each other.

'Thank you. I can manage the rest,' Nik murmured.

Alexandrie nodded. She placed his shirt on top of his jacket and left the room, sliding the door closed with a click. Nik clasped his mouth, staring at the door, his pulse racing from her touch on his skin. He stood wincing and hobbled into the bathroom.

———————

Sunlight spread across the room, rousing Nik to wakefulness. The morning sunbeams warmed the floorboards between the window and bronze-coloured curtains. He tried to read the digital clock set into the cushioned bed head and cursed out loud, his limbs and torso spasming with the effort of turning.

'Nikolaos, are you alright?' asked Alexandrie through the door.

Nik curled up on his side, waiting for the shooting pain to pass. He opened his eyes at the cool, gentle touch of her hand on his forehead, brushing back his hair. He took a few deep breaths, the throbbing subsiding.

'I'm going to call an ambulance,' she said, kneeling on the floor and peering into his eyes.

'No, it's easing,' he ground out. From the arch of her eyebrow, he knew she didn't believe him. He grabbed her hand and attempted a smile. 'As the doctor stated, I'm young and will recover.'

'That's not comforting, Nikolaos.' Her brows furrowed. 'You can't move. What if you have internal injuries?'

'The CT scans were clear. It's the bruising from being flung into a wall.' He squeezed her hand in reassurance. 'Next time, I'll remember not to get caught in a mini explosion.'

'That's not funny, and there is no next time,' she said, the lines around her mouth tightening. 'This is much too dangerous. I will continue the search with my team.'

'Not going to happen.' He locked eyes with her. 'If it wasn't for my information, you wouldn't know where next to track Ritterbusch. This was a freak accident. It could have happened to anyone, even to an experienced police officer like you. And then what? Your Interpol counterpart takes over the investigation, and I don't believe you would be too pleased if Janssens took the lead.'

Her brows scrunched in disapproval. 'You mentioned Ritterbusch may go to Madrid.'

'Yes, but you don't know which shops.'

'I'm confident I can find out which antique stores sell rare coins,' she pointed out, starting to get annoyed.

'Maybe, except there are quite a few shops in Madrid that sell coins, and I happen to know the ones Resnik owns.'

Alexandrie narrowed her eyes at him. 'If I couldn't protect you from the explosion, how am I to prevent anything else from happening to you? I have failed in my duty as a police officer.'

'It was an unfortunate incident that could have happened to anyone, even an experienced police officer. I absolve you of any responsibility for me throughout our partnership,' he said as he let go of her hand. 'If you don't mind, I would like to get changed now, so I can have breakfast and take those painkillers.'

She hesitated, stared at him for a moment and then stood in resignation. 'I will order room service.' She left the room, sliding the door closed behind her.

Nik gazed at the closed door and pressed a fist to his forehead.

His attraction for Alexandrie was something he did not expect. No matter how he tried to ignore his feelings, the more time they spent together, the more drawn he was to her. He sighed and stifled a groan as he got out of bed.

It took him forever to pull on his underwear and jeans, and he gave up on putting on a t-shirt. He padded out into the small living room where Alexandrie looked up at him and stared, the corners of her mouth twitching.

'It was too difficult to get the t-shirt over my head so I decided the jacket will do for now,' he said, chagrined. 'I will put on my t-shirt once I've eaten and taken painkillers.'

'You ... ah ... look like an Italian gigolo,' she said biting her lip, her tawny eyes twinkling.

He glanced down at himself. 'I'm glad my attire amuses you, anyway I now fit in with the Euro trend.'

She stifled a giggle. 'Such fashion was never a tasteful style and still is not chic.'

'Where's that breakfast?'

CHAPTER 36

Nik took the coin from his pocket and examined the profile of the turtle, turned it over and inspected the three running legs. His grandfather had explained the Trinacria meant movement. Given the special properties of the coin, Nik surmised, the symbol had much more significance than the action of moving. More so now, given the reaction the two coins had displayed when they were in close proximity. He assumed Ritterbusch was now aware of the second coin. From here on, Nik needed to be more judicious when using the coin. He picked up his phone and dialled a number.

'*Bonjour*, Nik.'

'*Bonjour*, Odette.'

'Is your detective still in Rome?' she asked with a slight edge in her voice.

'No, she left yesterday,' he replied, preoccupied with the coin and not hearing the accusation in her tone. 'Would you do a little research for me, please?'

'What is it you are looking for?' she asked.

'I'm not absolutely sure, whatever information you can find would be helpful,' he answered. He explained what he wanted.

'Is it to do with what Resnik is searching for?'

'Yes.' He set the coin on the coffee table.

'When are you coming home?' she asked.

He smiled at her use of 'coming home'. 'Today.'

'*Bon.*'

'Also, are you able to arrange accommodation with two bedrooms at a hotel in Madrid?' he asked.

There was no response.

'Hello, Odette? Are you still there?'

'When are you planning to go to Madrid?' she asked, her tone flat.

He replied in a resigned voice, 'In two to three days' time.'

'Is there anything else?'

'No. That's all for now, thank you.'

'*Adieu.*' She hung up.

Nik checked the safe once more, making sure he had emptied its contents, and did a quick scout of the bathroom and bedroom. He patted his side, comforted by the familiar weight of the gun underneath his jacket and the knife strapped to his shin. While the detective remained in the suite, he had kept both weapons and ammo locked in the safe. He didn't want to deal with the questions, knowing she would have confiscated them.

The room seemed hollow and quiet, and for reasons he couldn't fathom, he felt even more alone. The past day, even more so. He had convinced Alexandrie to leave, telling her that he was fine and they would meet to strategise on his return to Paris. She had been reluctant to let him travel on his own and on a motorbike. He pointed out that her boss would be wondering why she hadn't reported in and what she was doing in Rome. She left on the provision that he would contact her when he arrived.

He placed an envelope for the young footman on the desk near the door, grimacing as he bent to pick up his backpack. He tossed the coin.

Somehow, he was going to have to explain to Odette that he required a new motorcycle.

EPILOGUE
SLOVAKIA – KONRAD RESNIK'S RESIDENCE

Iasos sat slumped in the chair, puffs of condensation from his mouth the only sign he was still alive. His head drooped low, the bristles on his chin brushing the lapels of his jacket. He didn't notice the cold air in the room, his limbs blue and numb from sitting and being bound. The only relief he got was when he was escorted to the bathroom.

His eyelids twitched.

'Wake him.'

Iasos gasped. His eyes widened in shock and his body trembled as icy cold water sluiced his face and drenched his chest. The water pooled beneath his backside and at his feet. He drew in a ragged breath, tasting the mixture of blood and water in his mouth.

Resnik gripped Iasos's chin, squeezing tight, his pale blue eyes flinty.

'Your grandson has become a liability. He is following the same path you traversed in the search for the coin. Tell me what he knows.'

'He knows nothing,' Iasos snarled.

Resnik's fingers bit deep into his jaw. 'How does he know about the stores I own?'

'He doesn't. We discussed going to a variety of antiques shops before I left home.' Iasos glinted at Resnik.

Resnik snorted. 'I don't believe you.'

'It's the truth!'

'It's mere coincidence the coin stores he happens to visit belong to me?'

Iasos wrenched his jaw free and spat in Resnik's face. The Slovakian recoiled and staggered back. His henchman stepped forward and backhanded Iasos. The blow was hard enough to knock Iasos' head to the side, spittle and blood ejecting from his mouth.

Resnik wiped his face with a handkerchief as Ritterbusch strolled into the room. 'Track down his grandson, tell him I wish to arrange another meeting regarding his beloved grandfather. Bring a memento to encourage his decision.' He turned on his heel and exited, his henchman trailing after him.

'May the hounds of Hades rip you into shreds and feast on your bones, Pan Resnik!' shouted Iasos.

Ritterbusch punched him in the stomach. Iasos doubled over and gulped, the breath knocked out of him. The pain spread into his groin. He bit his lip, his eyes watering. This was not the way he wanted to depart the world, but protecting the coin was more important than his life and that of his family. His only hope was that Nikolaos's guardianship and the legacy of the coin remained a secret.

About the Author

Luciana Cavallaro is an award-winning author of historical adventure fiction that bends genres and reimagines myth. Her storytelling has been recognised internationally, with her books earning spots in major book and film competitions.

She began her journey as a storyteller at age three—behind the wheel of a car. (Her father never quite recovered.)

Discover more at https://lucianacavallaro.me/

OTHER BOOKS BY LUCIANA CAVALLARO

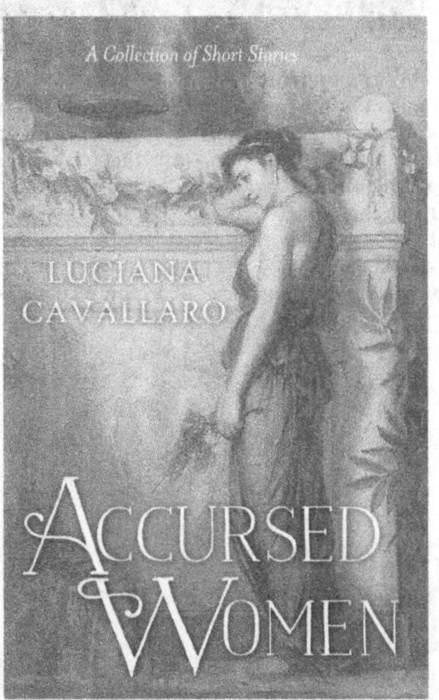

Five stories, five women, five legends. A Minoan Princess, a Spartan Queen, the Queen of the Gods, the first woman on earth and a Gorgone share their lives and stories in one volume.

Evan has been having some very strange dreams. The Perth-based architect dismissed an unexpected phone call from an entrepreneur in Greece, asking him to restore his family home, as the ravings of a crank. Until, that is, the dreams begin, each more vivid than the last. A dream encounter with a mysterious character called Zeus sees him catapulted back in time to 500 years before the birth of Christ. Evan finds himself quickly embroiled in a plot to prevent the birth of Christianity, an unwilling player in an epic struggle between the old gods and the new, fighting for his life.

Follow Evan as he continues his odyssey as Servant of the Gods in The Labyrinthine Journey. The quest to locate the sacred object adds pressure to the uneasy alliance between Evan and the Atlanteans. His inability to accept the world he's in, and his constant battle with Zeus, both threaten to derail the expedition and his life. Traversing the mountainous terrain of the Peloponnese and Corinthian Gulf to the centre of the spiritual world, Evan meets with Pythia, Oracle of Delphi. Her cryptic prophecy reveals much more than he expected; something that changes his concept of the ancient world and his former way of life. Will Evan and his friends succeed in their quest to find the relics and stop the advent of Christianity?

Evan and his companions are entrapped by the Amazon
Queen Antioche and her warriors. Memories and allegiances
are tested. The Dark Master's victorious revenge over the
gods is almost complete. The plight of the High Priestess is
precarious, her health ailing, and unable to rescue her brother
and fellow Atlanteans. The last sacred relic, secreted in the
lair of the Minotaur, must be recovered or the Dark Master's
succession plans of a new god are complete. The mystical
lands of Krete, the final stage of Evan's journey, are within his
grasp. He must succeed so his father, Zeus, fulfills his
promise. Then there is Queen Antioche, and the precious
gifts she presents him. Will Evan return home, and what will
become of his future? Minotaur's Lair is the third and final
book in the action-packed Servant of the Gods historical
fiction series. If you enjoy well-researched landscapes,
historic characters, excitement, mythical creatures and
unique settings, then you'll love Luciana Cavallaro's heroic
odyssey.

An ancient cover up, a dangerous legacy and the search for the most powerful object. A three-thousand-year old magical coin, the disappearance of an old man, fanatical neo-Nazis, and the hunt by Interpol, merge in this gripping story of an ancient cover up, and the transition of an ordinary man into the guardian of the most powerful coin on earth. High school teacher Nik Zosimos, leads an uncomplicated life until he receives a cryptic phone message from his grandfather, Iasos. He hurries to his grandfather's finding him relaxed and pleased to see him. A few beers later, Nik leaves his grandfather's place, stupefied and astounded. Iasos has a secret, one that dates back to the time of Herakles. But that was just a myth, wasn't it?

All books available from

www.lucianacavallaro.me

Amazon

Barnes & Noble

Dymocks